Praise for S

SPOILED

A *Slate* Best Book of the Year

"Thoughtful, surprising, and frequently hilarious."
—Laura Collins-Hughes, *Boston Globe*

"I can't recommend any Simon Rich book—especially this one—highly enough. From the hyper-competitive rituals of Scrabble players to the laments of a grieving, widowed hamster in an elementary school classroom, each story in *Spoiled Brats* opens with a brilliant comedic perspective that only gets funnier, more fascinating, more surprising, and more insightful from there. First-rate comedy with a heartbeat—this is one of my favorite books from one of my favorite authors."
—B. J. Novak, author of *One More Thing*

"Simon Rich, in his new collection *Spoiled Brats,* is in the *Blazing Saddles* phase of his writing career....As hilarious a portrait as you'll find of the self-involved, easily outraged, post-post-post-post-ironic world into which we've dumped the next generation....As solid a piece of comic writing as I've read in a long time."
—Patton Oswalt, *New York Times Book Review*

"I hate Simon Rich, the person. I love Simon Rich, the writer. This book is my favorite one of his yet."
—Charles Yu, author of *Sorry Please Thank You*

"A mix of gentle surrealism and smiley satire, the stories are bright, witty, occasionally tart, and just the right side of sappy."
—Sam Kitchener, *Telegraph* (UK)

"Rich brings new meaning to laugh-out-loud....His uproarious stories will undoubtedly have you nodding in agreement."
—Brittany Livingston, *Harper's Bazaar*

"Hilarious....Every story rings true."
—Joanna Burkhardt, *Library Journal*

"*Spoiled Brats* is ridiculous in the very best way....It mocks its protagonists without being mean; we find ourselves sympathizing and relating with these characters even as we laugh at them....*Spoiled Brats* is undeniably funny, but its real genius is that, like the best comedy, it encourages introspection as well."
—Carrie Rollwagen, *BookPage*

"At first glance, *Spoiled Brats* reads like Kafka with jokes, featuring conflicted chimps with father issues, synesthetic aliens, a deaf genie, and a twelve-inch pianist....*Spoiled Brats* takes aim at all our solipsistic delusions, resonating long after you've finally stopped laughing....A funny, smart collection."
—Sunil Badami, *Sydney Morning Herald*

"*Spoiled Brats* is brilliant, original, hilarious....An anthology as endlessly clever as it is hysterical....I could bore you with more superlatives, but why bother? There's no chance of buyer's remorse on a book this enjoyable."
—Matt Sedensky, Associated Press

Also by Simon Rich

Man Seeking Woman (originally published as
The Last Girlfriend on Earth)

What in God's Name

Elliot Allagash

Free-Range Chickens

Ant Farm

SPOILED BRATS

Stories

SIMON RICH

BACK BAY BOOKS

Little, Brown and Company

New York • Boston • London

Copyright © 2014 by Simon Rich
Reading group guide copyright © 2015 by Simon Rich and Little, Brown and Company

Back Bay Books / Little, Brown and Company
Hachette Book Group
1290 Avenue of the Americas, New York, NY 10104
littlebrown.com

Originally published in hardcover by Little, Brown and Company, October 2014
First Back Bay paperback edition, May 2015

Back Bay Books is an imprint of Little, Brown and Company. The Back Bay Books name and logo are trademarks of Hachette Book Group, Inc.

The publisher is not responsible for websites (or their content) that are not owned by the publisher.

The Hachette Speakers Bureau provides a wide range of authors for speaking events. To find out more, go to hachettespeakersbureau.com or call (866) 376-6591.

Portions of this book have appeared, in slightly different form, in Medium.com ("Elf on the Shelf") and *The New Yorker* / Condé Nast Publications ("Guy Walks into a Bar," "Family Business," "The Tribal Rite of the Strombergs," and "Sell Out"). "Semester Abroad" was originally published in Funny or Die's *The Occasional* © 2013, Funny or Die, Inc. All rights reserved.

ISBN 978-0-316-36862-9 (hc) / 978-0-316-36865-0 (pb)
LCCN 2014940627

10 9 8 7 6 5 4 3 2 1

RRD-C

Printed in the United States of America

For Kathleen

CONTENTS

ANIMALS

They buried my wife in a shoe box in Central Park. I like to imagine that the funeral was respectful, that her body was treated with a modicum of dignity. But of course I'll never know. I wasn't invited to the ceremony. Instead, the guests of honor were the students of homeroom 2K.

Her killers.

When the children returned from the burial, they drew "tributes" to my wife in Magic Marker—maudlin scribbles of halos, wings, and harps. It was hard not to vomit as Ms. Hutson taped them up above my cage. I've never seen such tasteless dreck in all my life.

Hailey, I noticed, was crying as she drew. The irony. It was her responsibility to refill our water bottle last week. Instead, she spent all her free time with Alyssa, practicing a clapping game called "Miss Mary Mack."

Miss Mary Mack, Mack, Mack!
All dressed in black, black, black!

It was that inane chant that provided the score to my wife's final moments. She was dying of thirst but never cried once. It was only later that I realized why: her body was too dehydrated to produce tears.

Pocahontas was her name.

My name is Princess Jasmine. I am a male, so this name is humiliating. But I'm aware that my situation could be worse. The other homeroom, 2R, has a guinea pig named Stimpy and an elderly turtle named New Kids on the Block.

Pocahontas left me with three sons, and it's for their sake alone that I keep up my struggle. Every weekday morning, when the monsters run screaming through the door, I hide my babies under scraps of newspaper. Whenever food and water are scarce, I give them my whole portion. Their faces are exact replicas of my wife's, and when I look at them, it helps me remember just how beautiful she was. Their names are Big Mac, Whopper, and Mr. T.

Mr. T was born with developmental problems. He was so small during infancy that we had to shelter him each night, wrapping our bodies around his shivering frame so that he could fall asleep. I've been through a lot. If I lose Mr. T, I'm not sure I'll have the strength to carry on.

It's morning now. The square of sunlight on the blackboard grows and grows. Soon the gremlins will run in howling, hopped-up on Pop-Tarts and primed for violence. For months, I assumed that this school was reserved for juvenile delinquents. But during Parent–Teacher Night, the mink coats and bespoke suits told a different tale. It turns out this school is a private one, an "elite" institution for the children of millionaires.

I can hear the nannies muscling their way through the lobby, dragging their little terrors toward my family. My sons are still asleep. I lick their faces and conceal them as best I can.

The bell clangs harshly. The nightmare begins.

Monday
8:25 a.m.

"What time is it?"

"Jobs time!"

My fur bristles as Ms. Hutson takes out the Jobs Board. This laminated poster, with its seventeen colorful squares, rules my family's existence. It determines everything: whether we feast or starve, live or die. I rub my paws impatiently while Ms. Hutson assigns the week's tasks.

"Pencil Organizer this week is... Dylan! Line Leader is... Max! And our two Table Wipers are... Kristen and Sophie!"

Eventually, she gets to the one job that matters.

"Hamster Feeder is..."

I scan the room. There are still some good candidates left. Maybe we'll luck out and get Caitlin? Last month she gave us double portions. If her name is called again, Mr. T might gain some weight in time for winter. It's while I'm enjoying this fantasy that Ms. Hutson clears her throat and—with one little word—sentences my family to death.

"Simon."

My eyes widen with horror. Simon Rich is 2K's "class clown," a pudgy, hyperactive boy with some kind of undiagnosed emotional problem.

"Hamster Feeder?" he shouts. "Whatchu talkin' 'bout, Willis!"

The other children laugh hysterically.

My God, I think. *This is it. This is how it ends.*

11:25 a.m.

"Free time's almost over," Ms. Hutson says. "Don't forget to do your jobs!"

I sigh with relief as Simon finally waddles to our cage. He doesn't feed us, though, or replenish our water. Instead, he picks me up by my tail, which is connected directly to my spine. The pain is so searing, it shocks me into a kind of perverse laughter. I did not know my body could hurt this way, that God would allow one of his own creatures to suffer on this level. Simon swings me through the air while singing nonsensically in his high-pitched nasal voice.

I glance at my babies, hidden safely under newspaper. Even at the peak of my agony, I am grateful that Simon has focused his sadism on me. Otherwise, it might be them who suffered.

Free time ends, and Simon drops me back into my cage—from several times my own height. My sons poke their heads through the newspaper. They look around confusedly, then stare at me in dismay. They're used to receiving food at this hour, but I have none to give. Simon has forgotten to do his one basic task. There is still some water left in our bottle from last week, but all it can do is prolong our agony. Without grain, we won't live long.

2:30 p.m.

During science class, Ms. Hutson unveils a large glossy map of the solar system.

"There are nine planets," she says. "Which one do we live on?"

"Mars!" Simon shouts. The other children howl uproariously. This is what passes for wit among them, the basic substitution of one word for another.

"Very funny," Ms. Hutson says, smiling indulgently. "But of course, we *really* live on Earth, the third planet from the sun. Mars is the *fourth* planet. And after that one comes Jupiter, Saturn..."

I sigh with misery. It's obvious what's about to happen.

"Uranus..."

There is a split-second pause, and then the class erupts into full-fledged mayhem. I try to shield my sons from the noise, but it's too late. The monsters have heard a "dirty word" and cannot contain their excitement.

"Uranus!" Simon screams. *"Your anus!"*

I lock eyes with the teacher, silently willing her to beat him. But all she does is walk across the classroom and turn off the fluorescent lights. Her strategy fails. The children's laughter grows so deafening that I can feel my eardrums throbbing in my skull. Some of the students are standing on their desks, swinging their arms around in a kind of mania.

The chaos gradually subsides, but only because the children grow exhausted. The utterance of the word *anus* has produced in them pure ecstasy. Several of them are crying real tears.

Ms. Hutson turns the lights back on, and I glance at the clock. The Uranus episode has lasted thirteen minutes. Before the lesson can resume, the bell rings. The spoiled brats run laughing through the door, another day of foolishness behind them.

I watch as my children drink our last remaining drops of water. We'll be lucky to make it through the night.

Tuesday
8:15 a.m.

I awake to the sound of screeching laughter. Sophie and Alyssa have made a dress out of pink construction paper and taped it to my sleeping body.

"You're a pretty girl, Princess Jasmine!" Alyssa says. "A pretty, pretty girl!"

I try to remove the costume, but the tape is double-sided and my paws are too weak to detach it. I must wear this "dress" indefinitely, in the presence of my own sons. I avoid their eyes and they avoid mine. Whatever dignity I had left is surrendered.

During attendance, everyone says "here" except for Simon, who says "*not* here." Somehow this gets a laugh. For the first time in my life, I think seriously about the option of suicide.

Ms. Hutson starts the day with a geography lesson. She spends ten minutes explaining the concepts of north, south, east, and west. Then she asks the class which country is "north" of the United States. The children stare up at her, completely baffled. Eventually, Jeffrey raises his hand. "Mexico?" he guesses. The teacher smiles at him encouragingly. "Almost!" she says. I watch in stunned silence as she hands the little moron a sticker, as a reward for "trying his best."

"What do we say," Ms. Hutson asks her other students, "when someone tries their very best?"

The children smile and break into a chant.

"That's all right, that's okay, we still love you anyway!"

I vomit bile onto my own legs. I've heard a lot of treacle in this classroom, but this new cheer is so cloying it pushes me over the edge.

The children continue to chant, their voices growing louder and more confident. It's no wonder they're such monsters. They've been taught that they're infallible, as perfect and blameless as gods.

You forgot to feed the hamsters? And brought about their deaths? *That's all right, that's okay. We still love you anyway.*

2:30 p.m.

During snack time, Simon and three other obese boys have a milk-drinking contest. It's hard to watch as they gorge themselves just inches from my starving children's faces.

Mr. T has begun eating newspaper to dull the pain in his stomach. My other sons sleep all day to conserve energy. For the first two days of our ordeal, I fantasized constantly about food. I hallucinated mounds of grain, piles of nuts, and luscious chunks of apple. Lately, though, I've stopped feeling hungry at all. It's as if my body has given up and braced itself for death.

Teddy wins the milk-drinking contest by downing seven cartons. He immediately throws up.

Ms. Hutson sends him to the nurse and calls for Carlos, the janitor. He arrives within seconds, carrying a tattered mop.

"*Hola!*" the children shout in unison.

Carlos is a native English-speaker, but the little racists assume that he is foreign-born.

"*Hola,*" Carlos says.

"I need you to take care of something," Ms. Hutson tells him, gesturing at the pile of vomit.

Carlos nods and gets to work. He's still scrubbing twenty minutes later when the final school bell rings.

"Adios!" the children shout as they run by him. "Adios!"

"Adios," he says, his eyes on his work.

Ms. Hutson peeks over his shoulder, her skinny arms folded across her chest.

"Are you going to disinfect the area?" she asks. Carlos forces a smile. He has already begun to disinfect the area but does not want to contradict her.

"Yes, ma'am," he says.

"I don't want that smell hanging around."

"Of course, ma'am."

When all the children are gone, she puts on some lipstick and changes into a pair of high heels.

"My dad's making me see opera," she complains.

Carlos nods awkwardly, unsure of how to respond.

"Don't forget to disinfect the area," she repeats on her way out.

Carlos finishes mopping and then walks from table to table, cleaning up after the fat beasts. *The Jobs Board is a total farce,* I think as he sponges up their filth. Kristen and Sophie are Table

Wipers in name only. At the end of the day, every job on the board belongs to Carlos. The only exception is Line Leader, which of course is a privilege that he will never get to enjoy.

Carlos looks at our cage and curses at the sight of all our feces. I avert my eyes with shame. I know we're not responsible for our prison's deplorable condition, but it's hard not to feel mortified.

As Carlos collects our soiled newspaper, I notice he has several tattoos on his forearm: a few cursive names and a large, ornate crucifix. I, too, am a Christian, although lately I've struggled to make sense of God's plan. I wonder if Carlos's faith is as battered as mine.

He refills our water bottle, and for the first time in days, I allow myself to feel hope. Before he can find our feed bag, though, Principal Davenport runs into the room.

"Carlos, there you are! A fifth grader shat himself in dance. Would you please take care of it?"

Carlos forces another smile and reaches for his mop.

"Of course, sir."

The principal gives him a thumbs-up.

"*Gracias!*"

Wednesday
10:45 a.m.

The water tastes so rich, it brings tears to my eyes. As I drink it, I can feel it coursing through my body, giving my parched veins life. I look over at my sons, asleep in their clean cage, their wet little noses twitching with contentment. Carlos has saved our lives. But for how long?

Mercifully, the children are gone this morning. They've been given a break from their arduous studies to enjoy a field day at Randall's Island.

The classroom is blissfully quiet until lunchtime, when the hobgoblins return. Their flabby red faces are streaked with grime and sweat. The smell is almost unendurable. Every child, regardless of fatness, has somehow won an athletic award.

"Boom shaka laka!" Simon shouts as he thrusts his golden prize over his head.

When he walks by my cage, I peek at the engraving on his trophy. PARTICIPATION, it reads. I wonder if Simon is aware that his trophy has no meaning, that all he participated in was a mass delusion.

"Great job, everybody," Ms. Hutson says. "That was some *great* teamwork today."

"Whatchu talkin' 'bout, Willis!" Simon says, and everyone laughs, including Ms. Hutson.

The children spend the afternoon playing with their awards. Simon comes up with the ingenious gag of holding his trophy in front of his groin, in an imitation of an adult penis. The other boys applaud him and rush to follow his example. The girls, meanwhile, busy themselves making "outfits" for their trophies out of construction paper. Ms. Hutson encourages this madness, passing out glue and jars of glitter.

Finally, at 3:15 p.m., the nannies come to take the creatures away.

"Don't forget to do your jobs!" Ms. Hutson cries. Simon doesn't even look in our direction. This makes three days straight without food. It's official: we are going to starve to death.

I glance at my sons. Their bodies still have breath, but I can see that something else has died inside them. Mr. T hasn't moved in hours. And this morning I caught Whopper leering at him with a look I wish I could block out of my mind. Taboos are breaking down. If food doesn't come soon, I know, we'll have to make our own.

Thursday
8:10 a.m.

As another hellish day begins, I gather my sons around me. I've rehearsed my speech all night, but it's still hard to utter the words. Eventually, with painful effort, I manage to force the terrible edict through my lips.

"If Simon forgets to feed us one more time...I want the three of you to eat my body."

Mr. T breaks down and weeps. But Big Mac and Whopper merely nod.

They know it's the only solution we have left.

I can hear Simon's voice before he enters the classroom, as piercing and abrasive as a siren.

"Whatchu talkin' 'bout, Willis!"

His use of this catchphrase has spiked in recent days. It no longer elicits the laughter it once did. In response, Simon has taken to screaming the slogan at full voice in the mad hope that volume might somehow restore the gag's appeal.

"Whatchu talkin' 'bout! Whatchu talkin' 'bout! Whatchu talkin' 'bout!"

He presses his face against the bars of our cage and chants the phrase, again and again, until the words bleed together and begin to lose their meaning. His noxious Doritos breath engulfs me, and I can feel the fury mounting in my chest. I think of the sound of my son weeping and the look my wife gave me as the last bit of life left her eyes.

"Whatchutalkin'boutWilliswhatchutalkin'boutWillis—"

I have only a little strength left. But it's enough to rise up and sink my teeth into the monster's flesh.

Friday
12:30 p.m.

"Words can't express how sorry I am. Safety is our top priority—I'm as appalled as you are that something like this could occur at our school."

"He had to get three stitches! The plastic surgeons say that the scar could be visible for months!"

I roll my eyes as Simon's mother starts to cry.

"He's just a little boy," she says. "And you let him be exposed to wild animals!"

I glance at my sons. They're still alive, but their breathing is shallow and erratic. Our cage has been moved to the principal's office, yet they don't seem aware of the change in our surroundings. "I'm considering pressing charges," Simon's mother prattles on. "My lawyer says I have a real case. Simon had to take a rabies test, and when the nurse pricked his thumb, he cried and cried. The doctor said he'd never seen a boy cry like that."

I smile proudly, thinking of this scene.

"He's going to need therapy," the woman continues. "Lots of it."

"Is there anything I can do," asks the tired principal, "to help regain your family's trust?"

Simon's mother turns toward our cage, her eyes narrowing.

"I want those animals out of the classroom."

Principal Davenport nods. "We'll move them to homeroom 2R."

"That's not enough," she says, her voice lowering. "I want them *destroyed*."

Principal Davenport clears his throat.

"Of course," he says.

He picks up a phone and calls for Carlos, who arrives within seconds, mop in hand.

"*Hola!*" the principal says. "Listen. I...uh...need you to take care of something."

I can smell the Dumpster before I see it, an overflowing bin of putrid trash. My nose begins to twitch as I process all the stenches: decomposing Dunkaroos and mold-encrusted Pop-Tarts; rancid, soggy Lunchables and spoiled Nestlé Quik. The monsters have accumulated so much waste this week, and now we're to be added to the pile.

"Sorry, little guys," Carlos says.

He scans the alley to make sure no children are watching. Then he pulls a hammer from his tool belt. I lick my children's faces one last time. I know my act of rebellion has hastened their deaths. But my guilt is assuaged by the knowledge that their suffering will soon be at an end.

Carlos holds the hammer over Mr. T's tiny skull. My son looks up, his eyes half lidded. I pray that he doesn't grasp the situation, that his final moments aren't consumed by fear.

"Sorry, little guys," Carlos says again. "Sorry."

He raises the hammer high, and his sleeve slides down his forearm, exposing his tattoo. He stares at the three cursive names. Then he puts away his weapon, grabs our cage, and runs.

Saturday
11 a.m.

I awake to the sight of three girl humans, gobbling pancakes and chatting rapidly.

"What do we name the babies?"

"Snap, Crackle, and Pop!"

"The mommy should be Mrs. Fluffy or Mrs. Furry or—"

"It's not a mommy," Carlos interrupts. "It's a daddy."

He pours some Cheerios into our cage.

"And we're going to call him Hercules."

All the girls laugh.

"Hercules!"

"*Why?*"

Carlos crouches down and looks into my eyes.

"Because he's tough. And strong. And he works long hours, even though it's a living nightmare."

His daughters look at one another nervously.

"Okay," whispers the eldest. "We'll call him Hercules."

Carlos clears his throat and wipes his eyes roughly with his sleeve.

"Good," he says. "Thanks. Now finish your breakfasts, every last bite. I mean it."

GIFTED

When the nurses handed me my son, I couldn't believe how perfect he was. Ben was so robust, nearly fifty inches tall, including horns and tail. Even the doula was impressed.

"My God," she said. "My holy God in heaven."

Alan and I knew instantly that our child was exceptional. He was just so adorable, with his pentagram birthmark and little, grasping claws. His red eyes gleamed with intelligence. When the doctors came in with all their charts, they just confirmed what we already knew. Our child was "one of a kind" and "unlike any creature born of man."

Alan and I were ecstatic—but also a little bit nervous. Raising a gifted child is a huge responsibility. And we were determined not to squander Ben's talents. We vowed then and there that we would do all we could to ensure he achieved his full potential.

The first step was getting him into the right preschool. We figured it would be a breeze, given Ben's obvious star quality. But, to our great surprise, he struggled with the interview requirement. At Trevor Day, a teacher asked him how old he was. Instead of saying "three," he gored open her stomach and then pinned her to the ceiling with his mind. We were able to get him an interview at Trinity, thanks to a family connection. But when Ben saw the crucifix in the lobby, his eyes turned black and the walls wept blood. Why was Ben behaving this way? There was only one logical explanation: attention deficit disorder. We took him to a specialist on Park Avenue, and within five minutes our son had his first prescription for Ritalin.

At first Ben wouldn't take his pills. Padma, our nanny, had to chase him for hours around the apartment, blowing incense in the air to try to scare him down from the ceiling. Sometimes we had no choice but to crush up the pills and slip them into his ram's blood. Within months, though, Ben got used to his medication. He became calmer, more alert, and far less murderous. He was a real joy to be around.

In some ways, Ben still lagged behind most children. He spoke only one word: *arrgh*. And he was unable to tie his shoes or blink his eyes. We didn't care, though. Because, by the age of five, he'd finally found an outlet for his gifts. Art!

Ben always had a creative temperament. He could grip crayons by his second birthday (which is very rare), and by the age of six he was drawing every day. His favorite colors were black and red. Sometimes, while composing a sketch, he would become so excited that his crayon would break apart in his claws and he would start to ram his horns against the wall as noxious steam emitted from his ears. If Ben's art supplies were taken from him, he would respond with so much violence that Padma would have to subdue him, using one of the sleeper holds she'd learned. It didn't take long for Alan and me to realize we had a true artiste on our hands.

One time, my friend Carolyn—whose daughter, Esther, is Ben's age—came over to our apartment for tea. When I showed her Ben's drawings, she was so impressed, her face turned pale. Her daughter was still doodling fluffy clouds and rainbows, and here was Ben, already sketching three-dimensional bone altars. Carolyn would never admit it, but I could tell she was a teensy bit jealous.

We decided to enroll Ben at Dalton, because of its emphasis on creativity. I wasn't going to let Ben's talent go to waste at some cookie-cutter public school where every child is forced into the same dull mold. I wanted him to have a chance to find himself.

The truth is, both Alan and I had secretly hoped that our child would be a "creative." We each harbored artistic dreams in our youth (Alan wrote poetry and I made collages). Our parents, though, discouraged us from pursuing "les arts." In their opinion, it was just too financially risky. I'm thrilled that I ended up at Synergy Unlimited, and Alan loves his job at the Globex Corporation. But even though we've made successful careers in business, there's still a part of us that wonders, *What if?* With Ben (who's five times more talented than Alan and I ever were!) we finally had the chance to answer that question.

Ben's time at Dalton was not without incident. He's incredibly unique—every teacher said so. But his creativity could sometimes be a burden. If a subject didn't "grab" him, he would have trouble focusing—and instead create a game of his own design. For example, in fifth grade, a teacher asked him to calculate the area of a four-by-six-foot rectangle. Instead of multiplying four by six, as a typical child might have done, Ben crab walked across the ceiling and blinded the teacher with a fire stare. A custodial worker was able to subdue Ben with a sleeper hold. But the incident was very traumatic for our son. Alan and I decided it was time to reexamine his treatment.

After consulting with our specialist, we chose to switch Ben from Ritalin to Focalin, which is a slightly stronger medicine. We also hired Han Cho, an astrophysics PhD candidate at Columbia, to tutor Ben five days a week after school. When I mentioned the tutor to my friend Carolyn, she said, "It must be nice to be able to afford help." I had to laugh. Ben didn't need "help." His teachers all agreed, in report card after report card, that he was "one of a kind" and "incredible." What Ben needed was someone to translate his ideas to the page. The sad truth is, our world is just not designed for differently abled children. Many assignments at Dalton require the use of pencils, which Ben cannot hold in his claw. Other projects involve calculators, which Ben considers food, or the use of English, which Ben cannot speak. Enlisting Han allowed Ben to complete his assignments at his own pace and in a way that showcased his distinct gifts. The implication that Han did anything beyond that is offensive and insulting.

Ben's grades soon improved. We were so grateful to Han for unlocking our son's potential that we started to hire him for weekends, too. We even took him with us to Greenwich every summer, so Ben could get a "head start" on the school year. Over time, Han became something of a big brother to Ben (although, of course, he was much, much smaller, physically). Once, they were studying vocab by the pool when I heard a loud splashing noise. When I went outside to check on them, Ben was holding Han upside down by the ankles and growling with delight.

"Help!" Han shouted, playing along with Ben's game. "I've lost control! I've lost *control!*"

One thing I find particularly interesting is that Ben never mentioned the fact that Han was of Asian descent. Many children Ben's age have problems befriending people from different racial backgrounds. But that's just not how Ben saw the world. He treated Han exactly the same way he treated everyone else in his life.

When Ben turned thirteen, and the pressures of his bar mitzvah were finally behind him, we knew it was time to start thinking about college. We met with a number of counseling firms before ultimately hiring Sterling Horizons, a small boutique company located near our weekend house in Greenwich. They helped us structure a four-year strategy for Ben that would demonstrate his skill set—and we followed the plan to the letter. By the time Ben was a senior, his résumé was absolutely glittering. He'd received five participation gavels from Model UN, been elected tri-captain of the Dalton golf team, and contributed numerous drawings to the school's *Fine Arts Magazine.* His GPA was a respectable 1.4, and even though he'd accidentally eaten several sections of his SAT he still managed to notch a 420.

Despite all of Ben's achievements, he did not seem excited about college. He'd spend hours in his room, playing violent video games and listening to moody, satanic music (I'll never understand today's bands—in my day it was ABBA!). The only time I'd see Ben was late at night, when he'd emerge from his room to raid the fridge for blood Popsicles. I worked to take advantage of these "sightings" as best I could. But when I tried to engage him in conversations about his future, he replied in typical teenage fashion, with a series of shrugs, grunts, and monosyllables.

"Do you want to go to a big school or a small school?"

"Arrgh."

"Do you want to be in a city or in the country?"

"Arrgh."

"Would you prefer lecture classes or seminars?"

"Arrgggh!!!!"

It was exasperating. In the end, we were able to persuade Ben to apply early to Bard. Alan and I had taken him there on a college tour and we were so impressed that we donated several tennis courts to their campus. When Ben was accepted, Alan and I were beside ourselves! But Ben wasn't as thrilled as you'd expect. Here he was, accepted into his dream school, and his smile was so faint I could barely see his fangs. It was obvious what had happened: Ben had burned out.

We met with Ben's psychiatrist and decided it would be best for him to take a "gap year." When I was growing up, this concept didn't exist, but it actually makes a lot of sense. The college process has grown so insanely competitive. By the time it's over, children need a chance to decompress. The only question was: where would Ben go? It was difficult to decide. He had his heart set on Transylvania, which I found baffling. (Italy would make more sense, since it has such a grand artistic tradition.) In the end, we compromised. Ben would spend two weeks on his own in Transylvania, as a reward for all his hard work. Then he'd spend six months at a wonderful program I found in Costa Rica that builds eco-friendly houses for the poor.

When Ben returned from his time abroad, he was a changed

man. He had a swagger to his step and a confidence I'd never seen before. Part of me wondered if he'd maybe met a girlfriend overseas, but I knew better than to ask. If there's one thing I've learned from my years as a parent, it's that the mother is always the last to know!

Unfortunately, though, Ben had trouble adjusting to college. He thrived within his major, creating dozens of "splatter" paintings in the Abstract Expressionist tradition. But he had difficulty with his core curriculum courses. Once, during a Spanish midterm, he escaped into the Hudson Valley woods and lived as a beast for several months, taking residence in a cave and eating neighborhood pets to survive. The local authorities were able to subdue him. And, thankfully, they turned him over to the Bard police, so that his outburst could be handled internally by the school. But the event was traumatic for Ben, and I decided it would be best for him to take a semester off. We also got him a prescription for Adderall, which is a slightly stronger medicine than Focalin.

It took nearly seven years, but Ben eventually earned his BA in painting. I'll never forget how handsome he looked on the podium, with his cute little horns poking out through his mortarboard. No sooner had he snatched his diploma, though, than my heart began to race. All I could think was, *What now?*

Ben moved back home and quickly settled into his old teenage routine, sleeping past noon and drinking blood out of the carton. After several long months, Alan and I were beginning to get nervous. One day, though, we read an interesting article in the *New York Times Magazine*. It was a very long piece, but the gist of it was this: *College alone does not prepare children for the modern workforce.* Writing papers and taking tests is all well and good. But if a kid is really going to succeed in the rough-and-tumble business world, he needs hands-on experience in his chosen field. Armed with this knowledge, I decided to hire the Apex Consulting Group (a small boutique firm that specializes in career planning). After several enjoyable meetings, they gave me their recommendation: Ben should intern with a working artist. When they told me this idea, I was so excited I could barely breathe. Finally, after decades of work, Ben would have a chance to fulfill his dreams.

When I told him the plan, he was so enthused he punched his fist through a wall.

"Aaaaaarrrrrgggh!" he screamed with obvious elation. *"Aarrrrrrrgh!"*

Apex Consulting introduced me to Jean Petis, an award-winning painter based in the Williamsburg section of Brooklyn. After I showed him Ben's portfolio and committed to buy a series of twenty-by-thirty-foot paintings, he agreed to take him on for a three-month period.

Ben's internship was not without incident. He gored some paintings, which Alan and I were forced to replace, and he did not get along with Jean Petis. After just four days, Ben quit his internship and disappeared into the Connecticut forest, where he lived as a beast for several weeks, drinking wild-deer blood to survive. I had to admit, part of me was disappointed. I'd trusted Bard to prepare my child for a career in the arts, and they'd completely "dropped the ball." I wondered if we had made a mistake by not seriously considering Oberlin.

After Ben was captured, we got him a prescription for

Kilmax, which is a slightly stronger medicine than Adderall. Then, on a rainy February morning, I sat down with him to talk about his future. As usual, it was difficult for us to connect.

"Do you think you'd like to try another internship?"

"Arrgh."

"Would you like us to rent you your own artist's studio in Williamsburg?"

"Arrgh."

The Kilmax, I noticed, had produced several troubling side effects. Ben's eyes—usually so bright and searing—had dimmed to a pale ocher. His horns were pointed downward and his fur was falling out in clumps. I was telling him about another option—the birthright trip to Israel—when he suddenly held up his claw, cutting me off midsentence.

"No...more."

I screamed for Alan, and he came running.

"Ben spoke!" I cried. We leaned in toward our son, keeping as still as possible. Ben gasped a few times, obviously struggling. Eventually, though, he managed to continue.

"No more...arrrrrgh! Pleeeeeaseeeeearrrrrgh! Me...not... sick. Me...arrrrrrrgh! Monster. Let...be...monster. Let be monster."

My eyes filled with tears. I'd always assumed that Ben would never talk—and now here he was, carrying on a full conversation! If Ben could master language, there was no limit to what he could achieve. I whipped out my iPhone and typed in Han's number from memory.

It was time to start thinking about law school.

SEMESTER ABROAD

September 23, 3014

Okay, so this is, like, my diary or whatever. I wasn't going to keep one, because it's sort of annoying to remember to do entries, but then I started thinking, *When Derek and I are old, we're going to look back at this time in our lives and be, like, "Wow,"* so I decided I'm going to speak into my transcriber every night before I go to sleep, unless I'm, like, you know, really wasted.

I guess I should start with the rocket launch. Derek came with me to the spaceport to say goodbye, which was really sweet of him, because he was halfway through a video game. And I was, like, "Long distance is going to be *so* hard, but I know we can make it work, because we're fully invested and we love each other," and he was, like, "Yeah."

The flight was awful. I had to put my phone away during lift-off, even though I was right in the middle of texting Derek. Eventually, the pilot said phones were okay, but by then we were in outer space, so when I took out my phone it kept floating around the cabin, which was, like, annoying. Eventually, I was able to finish texting Derek, but he didn't text back, not even after I texted him again and also left him a voice mail and some holograms. And I started to freak out, because my semester abroad had just started and things were already weird between me and Derek.

So then the pilot was, like, "If you go to the observation deck, you can see a view of Earth," and I really wanted to go, because seeing Earth from space is supposed to be this, like, transformative experience or whatever. But there's no cell reception on the observation deck, and so I couldn't go, because I was still waiting for Derek to text me back. He never did.

September 27, 3014

Okay, so, things with Derek have been really weird, but before I get into it, I guess I should talk about the program or whatever. I'm doing my semester abroad on Saturn, which I know is, like, pretty random. I was going to do Mars, but everyone was doing Mars, and I didn't want people to think, like, *Oh, she's only doing Mars because everyone's doing Mars.* So on the form I checked Saturn. Anyway, classes so far are pretty easy. It's a lot of Saturn history, which is super boring, but there's only two hours of lectures a day, and also the days here are two weeks long, so when you think about it, that's really not so much class time. On the weekends there are optional tours you can do to see what life is like among the aliens (sorry, I mean natives). I really want to do the tours, because I'm interested in other cultures and, like, that's one of the main reasons I'm doing a semester abroad, is to get perspective. But I haven't had time because Derek has been so weird. Which brings me back to things with him.

Okay, so, yesterday he finally sent me a hologram, but it was, like, only five seconds long and he did it at the dining hall, so there were, like, bits of people's arms and trays in it. And I was, like, if you can't take the time to go inside an orb and send me a private hologram, how is this ever going to work? But I didn't actually say that to him because I didn't want him to think I was being clingy or whatever. Anyway, I've decided I'm not even going to think about Derek for a while, because this is my semester abroad and it's supposed to be about me.

September 29, 3014

Tomorrow we have our first quiz. It's on the culture of the Narvians, who are our host tribe. I'm sort of nervous, because at Williams I get time and a half, and I'm worried that the teachers here won't know that I get that. Also, the reading is really confusing. The Narvians don't have any concept of "me" or "you" (they see their tribe as a "single living being"). It's, like, really hard to keep track of all the names.

Anyway, yesterday morning I sent Derek a text, to be, like, "I'm freaking out about the quiz," and I figured he would just ignore it, as usual. But he wrote back right away, saying, "You'll do fine," and I was, like, oh my God, that's *so* Derek. Just when I think he's a total jerk, he'll do something that's freaking amazing and I'll remember how much we love each other. In a way I think that this long-distance thing is a good test for us, because if we can get through it, it means we were really meant to be together.

Anyway, I was so relieved that things with Derek were finally good again that I signed up for one of the optional culture trips. We went to Titan, which is, like, the biggest moon. It's sort of cool, because it has all these underground rivers. But when I tried to text a picture to Derek, there was no reception. Like, *none*. So I complained to Narvia, who's, like, the alien lady who runs the program. And I was, like, "I don't want to be rude, but in the brochure it said there would be reception and I'm, like, trying to make long distance work with my boyfriend, Derek, and there's no reception." She tried to fix my phone by zapping it with her eyes, and it helped a little, but not really. And at this point I was sort of freaking out, because even though Derek can be a total jerk, I love him unconditionally, and I, like, for real want to have babies with him someday, and that's, like, actually something I think about, and I don't want it all to end just because of my stupid phone. So I was, like, "Narvia, what's going on with the reception?" And she explained that a war had started that morning between the Narvians (her tribe) and the Gorgons (who live on some other moon). It's complicated, but basically, when they have their battles or whatever, it screws up reception. So I was, like, "I know it's not your fault or whatever, but I just want you to be aware that there isn't reception."

September 30, 3014

So the quiz went okay, but I think I screwed up the last part because I was having trouble concentrating. Narvia made us turn off our phones for the quiz, so the whole time all I could think about was Derek and whether or not he was trying to get through to me.

Also, I was really, really hungry. That's the one complaint I have about doing a semester abroad: I'm interested in other cultures, and that's why I came to Saturn, to experience new things, but I'm sorry, the food here is ass. The Narvians don't eat meat, because they believe everything has "a common soul," and I respect that or whatever. But the fruits and vegetables here are totally weird. All they have in the cafeteria are these purple star-shaped thingies and these giant petals from different flowers. There's one vending machine in the hallway that has Nutri-Grain bars and that's what I've been living on this whole time. Also, there's no beer, only XanXan, which is made out of flowers (like everything here). I've tried it, and it's actually not horrible, but it makes you really hungover. I usually drink only on Thursdays, Fridays, and Saturdays, and today's Tuesday, but the quiz was so stressful and things with Derek are so weird that I think I'm going to make an exception.

October 1, 3014

Last night was the worst. I was doing XanXan shots alone in my room and watching *American Idol MXIII* on Hulu when I realized I'd forgotten to eat dinner. The thing is, though, you're not supposed to leave your pod at night, because that's when the Gorgons do their air strikes. I thought about waiting until morning to eat, but my stomach was, like, literally rumbling. And so eventually I was, like, forget it, I'm getting a Nutri-Grain bar. So I put on my suit and floated down the hall, but when I got to the vending machine, they were out of blueberry, which is the only kind I like, and all they had was strawberry, which tastes like straight ass. And this was just, like, the last straw. So I called Derek and he picked up, but he was acting really weird. And I heard voices in the background. And I was, like, "Are you at a party?" And he was, like, "No, I'm just hanging out with some people." And I heard some girls laughing, and I was, like, "Are there girls there?" And he was, like, "There are a lot of people here." And I was, like, "I thought you said it wasn't a party." And he was, like, "It's not a party."

So Narvia came by and was, like, "You must stay within your pod. The Gorgons are attacking."

And I was, like, "Listen, I know this isn't your fault, and I don't want to be rude, but in the brochure it said there'd be nightlife and there isn't any nightlife, like, at all." And she apologized and said that the war had escalated, and that the Gorgons had started enslaving and torturing the Narvians, and because of her antennae or whatever, she could physically feel it when her fellow Narvians were being tortured, because that's how her species has evolved. And I was, like, whoa, too much information, but of course I didn't say that, because I didn't want to be disrespectful of her culture. So anyway she made me go back inside my pod, but by that point Derek wasn't picking up his phone.

I would never admit this to anyone, but sometimes I wonder if Derek and I are even compatible. I mean, I love him with all my heart, and I know he loves me, even though he's never, like, said the words or whatever. But the thing is, we have pretty different interests. For example, he's really into full-immersion virtual-reality first-person-shooter games and I'm really into, like, relationships. That's the whole reason why I'm majoring in communications—because I want to work for a nonprofit when I graduate and try to save the world. I know a lot of people would say that's a crazy pipe dream and I should just give up, but I'm, like, you only live once and you have to seize the day. There's this quote I saw once on my friend Karen's yearbook page and I liked it so much that I put it on *my* yearbook page, even though I knew everyone would be, like, "You copied that from Karen," but I was, like, who cares, I like the quote. It goes: "Shoot for the moon, because even if you miss you'll end up among the stars." When I first saw that, I was, like, oh my God, I'm going to freaking cry, because I freaking love that. I try to talk about this kind of stuff with Derek, but it never works, because he doesn't like to have deep conversations. All he wants to do is play his video games and break his kill records, which are, like, really high, but so what?

I'm trying to decide now whether to text him good night. I kind of want to, because I miss him like crazy, but also part of me is, like, he doesn't deserve it, because I've sent him good-night texts for nine straight days and he hasn't written me back once. I don't want to play games, though, because I don't believe in them, so I'll probably just text him what I always text him, which is "Good night, XO, I love you."

October 10, 3014

Derek broke up with me. That's why I haven't been recording new entries, because it happened eight days ago, and since then I've just been crying.

I was taking a quiz when he called me up out of the blue. You're not supposed to use your phone in class, but Narvia was distracted, because there was some big Gorgon battle going on, and her eyes were rolled back in her head, so I was able to sneak out and take the call.

So the first thing Derek says is, "I want to talk to you about something," and my heart immediately starts pounding, because he never wants to talk about anything. So I'm, like, "What's up?" You know, trying to sound casual. And he's, like, "I think we should do an open relationship." And so I'm, like, "Where is this coming from?" And he's, like, "I don't think long distance is working." And so by this point I'm starting to get mad, because it's not *my* fault long distance isn't working, it's his for not making an effort. So I blurt out, "If you're going to be weird like this, what's the point of even dating, why not just break up?" and he says "Fine" and hangs up. And I'm, like, *Did what I think just happened actually just happen?* So I call him and text him and leave a voice mail and a hologram and I even send him a telepathic message, even though they're expensive and my plan doesn't cover them if I'm roaming, but Derek never responds. And finally I realize, *Oh my God, it's over. Derek Kleinbaum and I are no longer a couple.*

So for the next eight days, I don't leave my pod, not even to go to class, and eventually Narvia knocks on my door and I'm, like, great, just what I need right now. So I let her in and I expect her to lecture me about schoolwork or whatever, but instead she says, "Please pack your bags. The rocket leaves in one hour." And I'm, like, "What?" And she's, like, "Have you been listening to the bulletins?" And I'm, like, "No, Derek broke up with me."

And so she explains that the Gorgons won the war by rounding up all the Narvians and destroying them with a heat blast. And I'm confused, because she's a Narvian but she's still alive, and she explains that she survived because the lasers couldn't permeate the school, but all of her friends and family died. And I'm, like, "Oh my God," because that's freaking horrible. And I start to feel really bad, because all this time I thought we had nothing in common, but now that she's lost her tribe and I've lost Derek, and both of our worlds have come crashing down, I realize we're, like, exactly the same person.

So I'm, like, "I think it's time for some XanXan," and she waves her antennae like she doesn't want any, but I just ignore her and pour out two huge shots. And we start downing shots, like, one after the other, and I'm, like, "I know what will get our minds off things. Let's play 'Never Have I Ever'!" She doesn't know how to play, so I explain the rules and say, "You go first." And she's, like, "Never have I ever seen so great a genocide as the one the Gorgons inflicted on my people." And I want to be, like, *No, you're supposed to say fun stuff,* but I don't want to make her feel bad, so I just nod and take a sip.

We finish the bottle and I get on the rocket, and that's where I am now, just riding back home through space. And the pilot just said, "If you go to the observation deck, you can see a view of Earth." And I didn't look the last time, but this time I kind of want to look, because who knows when I'll get another chance? So I guess this is the end of my diary, because phones don't work up there. So I guess I'm just going to turn this phone off and go up there. Okay. This is it. I'm doing it. I'm turning this off. I'm going up there.

SELL OUT

I am not smart with words, but I work hard every day of my life.

When I come on boat I have only shirt and pants. The food is not kosher and I soon begin to starve. In middle of ocean, I trade pants for tin of herring. Is very cold without the pants. But I survive.

They send me to Brooklyn and I find job in pickle factory. Every day, I crawl through gears and pull out rats. Is not so easy. The rats have sharp teeth and do not like to be touched. But I work hard. When I start in 1908 they pay me eighty cents each day. By 1912 they are giving me ninety cents, plus bowl of potato soup.

I find beautiful girl named Sarah. Her left leg is lame since youth, but she has all her teeth. She is very clever and teaches me to spell words. I save up pennies all week long so on Sunday I can buy her treat, like seltzer or salt fish.

When we marry and she is with child, we stay up late each night whispering. We make great plans. We will have son, and he will have son, and so on and so on and so on. And someday years from now, when we are dead and gone, our family name will stand for strength and honor. Someday our hopes and dreams will come to pass.

One day at work I fall into brine and they close the lid above me by mistake. Much time passes; it feels like long sleep. When the lid is finally opened, everybody is dressed strange, in colorful, shiny clothes. I do not recognize them. They tell me they are "conceptual artists" and are "reclaiming the abandoned pickle factory for a performance space." I realize something bad has happened in Brooklyn.

The science men come and explain. I have been preserved in brine a hundred years and have not aged one day. They describe to me the reason (how this chemical mixed with that chemical, and so on and so on), but I am not paying attention. All I can think of is my beautiful Sarah. Years have passed and she is surely gone.

Soon, though, I have another thought. When I fall in brine, Sarah was with child. Maybe I still have family in Brooklyn? Maybe our dreams have come true?

The science man turns on computing box and types. I have one great-great-grandson still in Brooklyn, he says. By coincidence, he is twenty-seven years old, just like me. His name is Simon Rich. I am so excited I can barely breathe. Maybe he is doctor, or even rabbi? I cannot wait to meet this man—to learn the ending of my family's story.

"How about Thai fusion?" Simon asks me as we walk along the street where I once lived. "This place has these amazing gluten-free ginger thingies."

He gestures at crowded restaurant. It used to be metal factory.

"Are you a cilantro person?" he asks me.

"I do not know," I admit.

"Don't worry," he says. "There's a bagel place around the corner."

I sigh with relief and follow Simon into store. He orders two bagels with creamed cheese and hands me one. I cannot believe how large it is—like something to feed an entire Irish family. I take three bites and put the rest in coat, to save for supper. When I look up at Simon I see that he has somehow almost finished his whole bagel. He is eating so fast, I cannot understand it. It is like he is in race and must shove all the bread in his mouth or he will die. Between bites he gulps from his drink, which is bottle of green sugar water the size of bucket.

"Gatorade?" he asks me.

I am too repulsed even to respond.

Eventually, he has eaten all his food and swallowed all his sugars. I wait for him to catch his breath, but then I can wait no longer.

"Please," I say, "I must know. What path have you chosen for your life?"

Simon smiles proudly at me.

"I'm a script doctor," he says.

I shake my head with astonishment.

"That is so wonderful," I say, my eyes filling with tears. "I am so proud. I cannot believe my descendant is medical doctor."

Simon averts his eyes.

"It's actually just a screenwriting term," he says. "'Script doctor' means I, like, punch up movie scripts."

I stare at him blankly.

"'Punch up'?" I say.

"You know, like, add gags."

"What sort of gags?"

He clears his throat.

"Let's see ... well, the script I'm working on now is about a guy who switches bodies with his pet dog. So I'm adding all these puns, like 'I'm doggone mad!' and 'I've got a bone to pick with you!' You know, things like that."

A long time passes in silence.

"So you are not medical doctor."

"No," Simon confesses. "I am not."

Simon says he is happy I was brined. He has always wondered what it would be like to "hang out" with his great-great-grandfather.

"We're going to have a blast," he says. "Brooklyn has gotten so awesome, it's crazy."

I ask him if he knows what became of my Sarah. He shakes his head. He has worked very hard to research our family, journeying all the way to place called Ancestry Dotcom. But all he could find about Sarah was the address she shared with me in Williamsburg: 283 Bedford.

"That's an American Apparel now," he says. "But don't worry. You can stay with me for as long as you want."

He leads me down Atlantic Avenue. We pass many strange people wearing tight pants and circus mustaches.

"So," I say sadly, "if you are not real doctor, I assume you did not have real education."

"Oh, sure I did," he says. "I went to Harvard."

I am amazed.

"My God," I say. "Did they know that you were Jew?"

"It's pretty different now," he says.

"What did you study? Latin and Greek?"

"Nah, I was an English major."

I squint at him.

"I do not understand. You did not speak English before?"

"No, I spoke it."

"Then why did you study it? What was the purpose of that?"

Simon ignores me and gestures at large brown house.

"Here we are," he says, grinning. "Not bad, huh?"

I look up at building. It is enormous.

"Are you servant here?" I ask.

"No," he says, laughing. "I own the place!"

At this point I become suspicious.

"What other jobs do you have besides the dog gags?"

"None," he says. "I'm a full-time screenwriter."

Once again, I am confused. I have been with Simon all day. He clearly does not work "full-time," not even close. I explain this fact to him.

"Let's just go inside," he says.

Simon and I look very much the same. We are both tall (five feet seven) and have handsome bump in nose. There are differences, though. For example, his hands are very soft, like woman's. Also, his arms are weak and small. They remind me of baby I saw once who had the wasting sickness.

When I first move in with Simon, I do not really understand what it means to be "script doctor." But as the days go by, I learn about the job. The way it works is this: Each day, for twenty minutes, he sits down and types words. The rest he spends complaining.

"I'm so pissed off," he tells me one day. "They hired me to polish the new *Spy Donkey* sequel. But just looking at it, it's going to need a page-one rewrite. It's, like, I didn't sign up for this. You know what I mean, Hersch?"

I do not know what he means. But it is clear he is upset, because he is drinking so much alcohols in middle of the day.

"That sounds bad," I say, trying my best to be polite.

"It's *real* bad," he says. "There's no way I'm doing a whole fucking draft for them. It's, like, you gotta draw the line somewhere, you know?"

He refills his alcohol glass.

"You ever deal with this kind of bullshit at the pickle factory?"

I think about it.

"There was one time my friend got caught in the gears," I say. "And it ripped up his torso, through the chest. And there was blood coming out of his mouth and he was screaming. And I plead with them to stop the machine, because my friend is dying, but no one listens to me, and my friend keeps howling until he is dead. And for years I see his face inside my dreams, with the blood coming out of his eyes and his mouth, begging for me to please save him."

Simon says nothing for a while.

"Maybe I'll just do the draft," he murmurs.

One night we have dinner with Claire, a goyish woman Simon mates with in defiance of our Lord.

"So," she asks me, "where are you from originally?"

"Slupsk," I tell her.

"It's near the Poland–Lithuania border," Simon explains with big smile on his face. He is wrong, but I do not contradict him. He seems very proud of knowing this one fact about me.

"That's so cool you're from there," Claire says to me. "I've always wanted to visit Eastern Europe."

I fold my arms and squint at her.

"Why would you visit there?"

"I don't know," she says, shrugging. "I hear it's got a really cool art scene."

I lean in close to her.

"The only scene in Slupsk is people eating horsemeat to live and killing each other for potatoes."

I point my finger at her face.

"You must never go to Slupsk," I warn her. "It is city of death."

"Oh," she says softly. "Okay."

She stands up.

"I'm going to cut up the tofu."

"Thanks, honey," Simon says.

"You must never go to Slupsk!" I call out after her.

When girl is gone, I grip Simon's shoulder and stare him in the eyes.

"That girl is too thin," I say. "She has not long to live."

Simon chuckles.

"That's just how girls look these days," he says. "Here, I'll show you."

He opens thick, smelly book with shiny pages. It is magazine, he explains, called the *Vogue*.

"This model's famous," he says, pointing to mostly naked woman. "She was married to Orlando Bloom."

I squint at the picture. The girl is very pale, with vacant eyes.

"I have seen this disease in Slupsk," I tell him. "First, they cough the blood. Then they begin to shake. They ask for the water, but when you bring them some to drink, it makes them vomit up the black. They die screaming, their eyes wide open, afraid."

Claire returns.

"Who wants tofu?" she asks.

"Please," I tell her, "eat my portion."

One day, I wake up to the sound of yelling. It is Simon. He is kicking his foot against his desk, shouting profanities.

"Motherfucker!" he cries. "Fucking goddamned fuck!"

I jump up from couch and run down hall. It is clear Simon has experienced a tragedy—something monstrous, like the death of someone close. I get to his office and gently open door. Simon is sitting at his desk, shaking his head and massaging his temples. His skin is pale and he is out of breath from screaming.

"Goddamn Internet's down," he says. "Second time this morning."

"What is Internets?" I ask.

"It's a thing on computers."

"What is computers?"

It takes him long time, but eventually Simon is able to explain. A computer is a magical box that provides endless

pleasure for free. Simon is used to constant access to this box—
a never-ending flow of pleasures. When the box stops working—
or even just briefly slows down—he becomes so enraged that
he curses our God, the one who gave us life and brought us
forth from Egypt.

"It's Time Warner," he tells me. "They're the fucking worst."
He bangs his fist against his desk.

"How am I supposed to get work done without the Internet?"

I glance at his computer machine. I am still learning about
modern technologies. But I am pretty sure from looking at it
that Simon has not been doing "work." There are three boxes
open on screen. In first, there is sports scores. In second, there is
pornographies. In third, there is Simon's own name, typed into
thing called Google.

Simon notices me looking at his computer and quickly steps
in front of it.

"I was taking a break," he says, his voice loud and defensive.
"You must have taken breaks sometimes at the pickle factory."

"Is true," I say. "Whenever there was fire, we would get to
leave factory until they finish clearing out the dead."

His phone begins to play loud song.

"I'm sorry," he says. "I gotta take this, it's my agent."

He picks up phone and paces around office, a pained look in
his eyes.

"I already said no to that!" he says. "No—I don't want to
punch up any more sequels. Because it's completely unfulfilling.
It's someone else's characters, someone else's plot—I'm supposed to be working on my novella."

He pauses midstride.

"They're offering *what?* For just six weeks? Holy shit."

He continues to pace, but slower, and with a strange look in his eyes. It reminds me of time I saw hurdy-gurdy man get hit by brick. He was very embarrassed, and also in pain (because the brick had been thrown into his genitals). But his desire for moneys was so great, he continued to play his song and try to dance his jig.

"You know what?" Simon says in as cheerful a voice as he can make. "That's actually an excellent idea for a *Zoo Crew* movie. I mean, they already had Captain Cow go to outer space in the fifth one. But he's never been to the *moon.*"

His voice lowers.

"Do you think we can get them to go up even higher? No? Okay—just checking."

He puts away phone and we make eye contact.

"What are you looking at?" he asks.

"I am just standing here," I say.

That night Simon's goy comes with giant bag of vegetables.

"I heard you're into pickling," she says. "So I went on Epicurious and planned a pickle-themed menu. We're having broiled trout with pickle butter—and a pickle-vinaigrette salad on the side."

In truth I despise eating pickles, because they remind me of the deaths of many friends. But I do not want to be rude.

"It is generous," I say.

"It's nothing," she says. "I want us to become better friends, you know?"

She takes out an onion and begins to chop it, very slowly, in an incorrect way. When Sarah chopped vegetable, she used big, heavy knife. She would hold one end down and then swiftly lower blade like it was lever. Claire chops onion using tiny, skinny knife, making one little cut at a time. We will not eat for many hours.

"I've been meaning to cook more," she says. "Simon likes to go out every night. Between you and me, I'm getting pretty sick of it."

She is barely halfway through the onion when the knife slips and slashes her finger.

"Fuck!" she screams. "Ow, fuck!"

She starts to cry as her blood seeps onto counter. Suddenly, I hear the sound of another woman shriek. I spin around and am surprised to see that it is Simon, standing there with his hands over his eyes.

"Oh my God!" he shouts. "Your fucking finger!"

"What do I do?" Claire cries. "What do I do, what do I do?"

"I don't fucking know!" Simon sobs. "Fuck fuck fuck!"

I sigh and grab girl's hand. She resists me, so I must shush her like a child.

"Is fine," I say. "Is baby cut."

I pour liquid soap over her finger and run faucet. She screams and I have to shush her again.

"Is fine," I say again. "I fix."

I grab a rag, rip off strip, dry her cut, tie the wound, and pull.

"There," I say. "Is better."

Claire slowly catches breath.

"Thanks, Herschel," she says.

Simon sighs loudly and steps out from the shadows. Somehow, at some point, he has poured himself giant glass of alcohols.

"Well!" he says. "Glad that's behind us. How about we grab some tapas?"

He is starting to put on coat when Claire waves arms.

"We can't," she says. "I planned out a whole meal for Herschel."

Simon squints at her. "But your finger's all fucked up."

"It's just a baby cut," she says, smiling wide at me. She has all her teeth, I notice, just like Sarah.

Even though Claire is bad at cooking, and believes in false god, and dresses like prostitute, with both ankles exposed, she is not so stupid a person. I know this because she is always reading books. I have read books before—a red one and also two blue ones—so I know a little bit about it. But Claire's books are much larger, with hard covers and pages filled with numbers.

"She's getting a PhD in sociology," Simon explains when I ask him about it. "Over at Columbia."

"What does she read so much about?"

"Something with immigration reform, I think? To be honest, I kind of tune out when she starts blabbing about it. It's a pretty boring thing to study."

This comment is strange, I think, coming from man who studied English in college—a language he already spoke. But I say nothing.

One afternoon, I am mending shirt in living room when Claire enters, wearing pack on back.

"Mind if I study in here?" she asks.

"Is fine," I say.

It takes her long time to spread materials onto table. There is pencils, papers, books, ruler, electric number machine, erasing stick. The last thing she pulls out is the strangest: it is terrifying golem with wrinkled face and purple hair. She notices me staring and smiles.

"That's my lucky troll doll. I've studied with it since middle school."

"Is it from witch?"

"I think it's from Kmart."

I pick up and examine, making sure not to look into its eyes.

"Simon's always making fun of it," Claire says.

"That is madness," I say. "He is asking for curse."

She laughs for some reason and opens up her book. Before she can start studying, though, Simon enters, holding his computer.

"Read this," he commands, plopping it onto her lap. "Tell me if it's funny."

"I'm kind of swamped," she says. "Is it okay if I read it tomorrow?"

"Sure," Simon murmurs. "No problem."

He groans like he is in pain, and reaches very slowly for his computer.

"Okay, okay," Claire says after a few seconds of this. "I'll read it."

I watch as Simon begins to pace the room, his baby arms

shaking at his sides. Every few steps he glances at Claire, to watch her face.

Eventually, she looks up from the screen.

"It's funny," she says.

Simon glares at her. "You didn't laugh."

Claire hesitates.

"Well...maybe it's not *laugh-out-loud* funny..."

Simon moans into his hands like a man who has lost his family. Claire hops out of chair and begins to stroke his back.

"Simon, it's great!" she says. "The part where the cow gets Auto-Tuned? That's going to kill."

Simon peeks out between his fingers.

"You don't think it's cheap?"

"No!" Claire says. "It's great! Really, really...great."

I notice that she is using the word *great* a lot. It reminds me of when my boss gave me tour of pickle factory. He kept using the word *safe.* "These gears are very safe," he would say. Or, "That belt is perfectly safe." The more he said the word *safe,* the more I started to think that things were maybe not so safe.

"It's *great,*" Claire says again. "The studio's going to love it."

"Really?" Simon asks, his voice high-pitched like a girl's.

"Yes!" Claire says, smiling as wide as she can make her lips go.

Simon sighs with relief.

"Okay," he says. "Great."

He grabs his computer, knocking down troll by mistake. When he is gone, I shoot Claire a look.

"He is asking for it," I whisper.

She laughs as I set her troll uprighs.

*   *   *

On Friday evening, I comb my hairs and knock on Simon's door. I am surprised to see that he is mostly naked.

"What are you doing?" I say. "It is almost sundown. We have still not said our Shabbos prayers of thanks."

Simon does not look in my direction.

"I'm busy," he says.

"God commands us to rest on Shabbos."

"Herschel, I've gotta turn this in by five p.m. L.A. time."

"But it is Shabbos."

"Dammit, Herschel!" he says. "I know religion's a big part of your life, and I respect that or whatever, but it's not a part of mine. I don't even believe in God."

I am so shocked it is difficult to breathe. I did not say anything when I learned that he ate bacons, and did not own yarmulke, and spoke no Yiddish (except for several words that all mean *penis*). But to learn that he has lost faith in our God — despite all the blessings in his life — it is too much to bear.

"How do you get through your days?" I whisper. "How do you find meaning?"

He thinks for a while.

"Through my art," he says finally. "That's how I find meaning. Okay? Through works of art."

I squint at the script he is working on.

"What is *Penguin President*?"

He averts his eyes.

"I don't want to talk about it."

I grab the script and throw it at his chest.

"No, I want you to!" I say. "I want you to tell me about this art you do that is so meaningful it would make you miss the Shabbos!"

He flips through his script and sighs.

"It's about a penguin who becomes president."

I squint at him with confusion.

"How would this happen?"

"He wins an election."

"So he is able to speak, this penguin?"

Simon throws up his hands in frustration.

"Do you really want to know? Or are you just trying to make me feel bad?"

"Yes," I say. "I want to know how this penguin becomes the president of the country."

He sighs again.

"He wins a break-dancing competition on the Internet."

"That makes no sense."

"You think I don't fucking know that?" he shouts, throwing the script down on the floor. "I told them in six meetings that it didn't make any fucking sense, but they won't listen, Herschel! They want the penguin to break-dance in *every scene*. In the Oval Office, on *Air Force One*..."

His voice begins to break.

"The penguin's always break-dancing."

I put my arm around his shoulder.

"Maybe you should quit this horrible work?"

"Herschel, it's not that easy," he says. "They're paying me thousands of dollars. I can't turn down that kind of cash, especially when I'm trying to save up for a house."

I am confused.

"You already have house."

"I know," he says. "But a bigger, wider one just went up for sale down the block."

He points out the window. There are many brownstones everywhere, but I have no idea which one he means. They all look exactly the same.

The next day Claire runs into house, laughing and shouting.

"I'm finished!" she shouts.

"Finished with what?" Simon asks, his eyes still on his computer.

Claire crosses her arms, then marches upstairs.

"Her final exams," I explain to Simon.

"Oh, right," he says. "Fuck."

He runs up after her.

"Honey, I was just kidding! Congratulations! Let's celebrate!"

I hear some arguing, followed by the sound of Simon pleading. Eventually, he persuades her to come back down the stairs. She has put on shiny shirt, I notice, and painted her eyelashes black.

"Better get dressed, Herschel," Simon says. "We're going to hit the town!"

"I am dressed already," I say. "My shirt is mended. I am ready to go."

Simon bites his lip.

"You know, Hersch, I was thinking, maybe you'd like to try another outfit for a change? I've got some old Ted Baker stuff I bet would fit you."

"I am not one who takes charity," I say. "My shirt is mended. Is *fine*."

"Okay," he says, waving his hands in the air. "Just offering."

He heads for the door, and Claire and I follow. We are almost out of house when Claire suddenly spins around.

"Oh no," she says. "I forgot tomorrow's Sunday."

"So?" Simon says.

"The maid's coming."

Simon groans.

"Honey, the place looks fine."

Claire kicks off her shoes and runs downstairs.

"Just give me a second!"

"Fuck," Simon says when she is out of earshot. "This is going to take forever."

I hear the sound of mopping in the kitchen.

"I do not understand," I say to Simon. "Why is Claire cleaning if you have hired maid?"

"Because she's nuts," he says. He opens wooden cabinet and pours out glass of alcohols.

I can hear more sounds from kitchen—the stacking of plates, the scraping of pots. Eventually, Claire comes upstairs, holding yellow sponge.

"You can save a little work for Hong," Simon tells her.

"Her name is Hahn," she says. "And I'm just doing the low surfaces, because of her back."

I am very confused about what is happening, but I say nothing. The mood is tense and I do not want to get involved with things. Simon checks his watch as Claire finishes sponging the tables. By the time she is done, he has drunk his entire glass.

"Ready now?" he asks.

Claire sponges wet spot where Simon has spilled some liquor.

"Ready," she says.

Simon pauses in front of automobile and stares at his reflection in the window. He is wearing purple scarf with fancy tassels.

"Where are we going?" I ask him.

"Cabin," he says, running fingers through his hair. "It's the best bar on the Lower East Side."

"Can't we just go to Fontana's or something?" Claire asks. "There's going to be a huge line."

"Nobody goes to Fontana's anymore," Simon says, wrapping the scarf tighter around his neck. "Cabin's way cooler."

"How cool is this cabin that you need scarf?" I ask.

Claire laughs for long time. I do not understand it.

"Come on," Simon says, grabbing Claire by the wrist.

I follow them down Avenue A. The Lower East Side, I notice, has not changed much in one hundred years. The women are still emaciated and dressed in rags; the men still wear beards and have sad eyes.

Eventually, after checking purple scarf in two more windows, Simon brings us to the bar that is called Cabin.

"There it is," he says, a look of reverence on his face.

I squint with confusion at the small establishment. It looks the same as all the others we have passed. The only difference is that there is red rope in front of it, guarded by scary Negro giant.

"Hey, man," Simon says to him. "Cool if we go inside?"

"Sorry," the giant says. "Private party."

As soon as he says this, three men with greased hair appear. The giant steps aside, allowing them to enter. Simon curses under his breath.

"What is this place?" I ask Claire.

"Just some celebrity hangout," she says.

"What is celebrity?"

"It's, like, somebody people celebrate, because they're doing something special with their lives."

"Is Simon celebrity?"

She hesitates.

"Kind of? I mean...you know, in some circles...he's sort of well known."

I turn toward Simon. He is pleading with the giant, his hands clasped tight like a beggar's. He does not look to me like celebrity, but what do I know about it?

Claire starts to shiver, and I soon become worried. As I mentioned before, she is very thin and extremely close to death. It is not good for her to stand outside in cold, dressed in nothing but her prostitute clothes. Her arms are naked almost to the elbow. I start to wish that I had worn my wool so I could give it to her.

"Simon!" I shout. "You must give the woman your scarf!"

Simon turns his back to us. It is obvious he is pretending not to hear me, so that he can continue to wear scarf.

"I do not understand," I say. "What is his thing with that scarf?"

She takes deep breath.

"He got it in London," she says. "He's so obsessed with it he won't even trust me to hang it up for him. He says it's his 'trademark.'"

Simon trudges back to us with big forced smile on face.

"Just give me a few more minutes," he says. "I'm making inroads."

He is adjusting his scarf yet again when his eyes suddenly widen.

"Hey, it's B.J.!"

He points at the bar's entrance with both hands. A handsome man is leaving bar to smoke with beautiful woman.

"Who?" I ask.

"B. J. Novak," Simon says. "He's an actor—we go way back."

He hustles down the alley and throws arms around this B.J.

"What's up, buddy?"

The actor smiles nervously. It is clear he does not know Simon and is frightened.

"Remember?" Simon says. "We met in L.A. last year. During the table read for *Ice Chimps*."

B.J.'s face turns red as the beautiful woman starts to laugh.

"You were in *Ice Chimps*?" she asks, her little nose wrinkling with disgust.

"Just a cameo," B.J. says.

"He played Wayne Chimpsky!" Simon tells her. "He was *hilarious*."

B.J. forces a smile and pats Simon on the shoulder.

"So great running into you," he says. "I think we're going to head back inside."

"Sweet!" Simon says. "I'll come with."

The next thing I know, Simon is following them back into the bar, his arms around them like he is their friend.

"This guy with you?" the giant asks the B.J.

"I guess," the actor mutters.

Simon grins with pride as the guard steps out of his way. He is almost through the door when he remembers we are with him.

"Quick!" he whispers.

We scurry in beside him, like rats across a gangplank.

"See?" Simon says as we shuffle through the crowd. "Piece of cake!"

"Where?" I ask. I have not eaten dinner and am hungry.

"It's just an expression," Claire explains. "It means *easy.*"

"So there is no cake."

"No," she says. "I'm sorry."

"Is fine," I say.

We sit down at table in the back. It is next to the bathroom and covered with filth. I find the least disgusting chair and draw it out for Claire.

"So," I say, "tell me, how was the exam?"

"It was really hard," she says. "On the last essay, with five minutes left, I realized I'd forgotten to mention the Perkins Report."

"What is Perkins Report?"

"It's, like, the statistical backbone of immigration-reform theory. Somehow I'd forgotten to incorporate it."

"That's awesome," Simon says.

We swivel toward him. He is facing the bar, his pupils darting back and forth in obvious search for celebrities.

"That's awesome," he says again. "Hey—who wants a Manhattan?"

"I'll just have a beer, please," Claire says.

"Gotcha. What about you, Hersch?"

"I do not drink alcohols," I remind him.

"Gotcha."

He gets up from table and heads for the bar, his purple scarf fluttering behind him like a tail. I try to speak more with Claire, but it is impossible. The person in charge of the music machine has gone crazy. He is playing two records at the same time, mixing the songs together so that it all sounds horrible. The room is so loud and crowded, it reminds me of when I was in steerage. I wanted to survive, but there also was a part of me that prayed for the sweet release of death. Eventually, Simon returns with the liquors.

"Sorry that took so long," he says, handing Claire a murky brown drink.

"You wanted a Manhattan, too, right, sweetie?"

I can see she is annoyed. She swallows her drink, grimaces, and then goes to the bar by herself. By the time she returns, holding beer, Simon has launched into story about *Ice Chimps*. I cannot understand most of his words, but the gist of it is that, years ago, he said a joke at a table and a famous man laughed at his joke. That is his whole story. But it takes him nearly fifteen minutes to say it. For the first time since meeting Simon, I start to wonder if he is possibly retarded. He talks like my cousin Moishe, who was born with triangle head. His stories go on forever and have no meaning.

Simon is about to tell another story about his beloved *Ice Chimps* when a tall goy with long tie walks over to our table. I can tell he is drunk, because he is swaying back and forth and has red cheeks.

"Hey, girl," he says to Claire. "How's your night going?"

Claire ignores the stranger, but he sits down next to her as if they are intimates. I quickly move aside, so that Simon can confront the man. But to my great surprise Simon does not seem to notice the drunk's brazen insults.

"What's your name?" he asks Claire. He is smiling, but there is violence in his eyes.

"I'm having a drink with my boyfriend," Claire says.

The man laughs.

"Doesn't mean you can't tell me your name."

I look at Simon. He has picked up an alcohols menu and is squinting at it.

"I'm in finance," the man slurs. I notice that he has inched closer to Claire. Their legs are almost touching. I nudge Simon, but he continues to stare at the alcohols menu. It is at this point that I realize what is happening: Simon sees the drunk but is pretending not to—so he can avoid combat.

"I asked you for your name," the drunk says again. "What's the matter? You deaf or something?"

He lays his hand on Claire's thigh as if she is his wife. She glances at Simon, her eyes wide with panic. Simon's arms are twitching slightly and his jaw is clenched with fear. But his eyes remain fixed on his little menu.

Now, I am not the bravest person. As boy in Slupsk, I was afraid to wrestle bears, and only sometimes wrestled bears. And once, when doctor knifed out my appendix, I asked for aspirin pill. But I cannot just sit there while a man dishonors woman.

I lean across the table so the goy can see my eyes.

"She does not want to socialize with you," I say.

He laughs once more, his moist lips curling into grin.

"Who the fuck are you?"

"She does not want to socialize," I repeat. "Please leave our table."

At this point, Simon has no choice but to look up from his drinks menu. His face is pale with fear.

"Herschel," he whispers. "Calm down."

I ignore him.

"Leave our table," I tell the drunk again. "Or I will violence you."

The drunk reaches across the table and grips my shoulder.

"Do you have any idea who you're fucking with? My friend owns this place."

"Leave our table," I say again. "Or I will violence you."

The man laughs out loud, and I sigh. I do not enjoy fighting, but sometimes there is no choice. I punch the man's face, throw him on ground, kick his face, punch his head, and smash glass into his head. There are some screams and then the Negro giant throws me out the door. My brain hits ground and I lose time. When I wake up, Claire is kneeling beside me.

"Are you okay?" she asks.

I am in some pain but manage to make smile.

"Is fine," I say to her. "It was pieces of the cake."

★   ★   ★

That night, on couch, with bag of ice on head, I realize something: I have stayed in Simon's home for one week's time and still have not contributed to household. I have never been one to live on handouts. Enough is enough, I decide. It is time to make things right.

I go to Simon's office, find pencil and paper, and make list of consumptions. It is very upsetting to see it written out. In just seven days, I have eaten four pieces bread, half jar of sour cream, and two canned tunas. I have also bathed three times, twice with cold water and once with warm. Plus, of course, I have taken pencil and paper, to record all these debts.

I go through the items line by line and write down guesses at the prices. When I add it all up, it comes nearly to one dollar.

I search my pockets, but all I can find is seven Indian pennies. Outside, the sun is rising. I go to the kitchen and wait for Simon to wake.

Six hours later, he enters. He is naked except for underpants and undershirt, which reads, DALTON HOMECOMING CLASS OF 2002. He turns on his coffee device and stares at it.

"Come on," he says to the machine as it brews coffee for him automatically. "Let's *go*."

In about ten seconds the pot is full. He exhales with relief and pours its contents into giant vessel.

I figure this is as good a time as any. I clear my throat, take out my list, and start to explain about my debts. Before I can get any words out, though, he waves his hand in my face.

"Herschel, please, don't talk to me right now. I've got a splitting headache."

He is drinking out of coffee bucket when Claire enters kitchen.

I gasp. She is almost completely naked, in underclothes that expose both of her calves. I face the wall and close my eyes to give her proper privacy.

"It's okay, Hersch," she says, laughing. "You can look."

I turn around very slowly. Claire's shirt is bright red, the color of fancy French lipstick. Over her chest, words spell out CLAREMONT RIDING ACADEMY. I can see her entire forearms, all the way up to the elbows.

"My God," I whisper.

Claire giggles—and I feel my face swell up with blood. Simon glares at both of us and finishes his coffee.

"You were saying?" he grumbles at me.

I clear my throat and look down at my list.

"It is generous of you to house me," I say. "But, as I have told you, I am not one who takes charity."

"It's not charity," Claire says. "We love having you around!"

"Yeah," Simon says. "We love it."

I watch as Claire opens the cupboard and reaches for mug on top shelf. As she stretches to grab it, her red shirt climbs slowly up her body. I turn away as quickly as I can, but it is too late. I have seen the nude small of her back. My throat goes dry and for long time I cannot breathe. How could Simon allow her to parade in this way? It is very hard to continue speaking like nothing strange has happened, but somehow I manage to keep going.

"I have decided to search for new job," I announce. "When I

have savings, I will repay you for the breads and creams I have eaten, and rent myself a home of my own."

Simon laughs out loud.

"Good luck with that," he says.

"Thank you," I say. It is nice, I think, for Simon to be so supportive, given that we have had some problems.

"I was being sarcastic," he says.

I squint at him with confusion.

"I do not understand," I say. "You do not think that I will have success?"

Simon refills his coffee vat and smirks.

"Who's going to hire you? You've got no education, no experience, no skills."

"Simon," Claire says, "that's rude."

"It's not rude," he says. "It's realistic. I mean, for God's sake, Hersch, you barely even know how to speak English."

My face begins suddenly to burn. It is painful to hear my great-great-grandson say these things. I know I am not so clever. I did not go to kindergarten like a fancy man. But I am not as worthless as he says.

"I have experience with pickling," I inform him.

Simon laughs again, and I can see his teeth glinting in the light. They remind me of rat's fangs, their tips caked with yellow clumps of food. I know he is related to me, but I feel like he is different species. For first time all week, I am thankful that Sarah is gone. I would not like her to meet this creature, to see what has become of our shared dream.

"If you want some cash," Simon says, "I've got plenty."

He opens a drawer, pulls out a wad of banknotes, and tosses

them in my direction. I let the bills flutter to the floor. By this point, my whole face is tingling.

"I told you," I say through gritted teeth, "I am not one who takes charity."

"Well," Simon says, "you better get used to it. Because it's the only way you're going to survive."

My jaw clenches tight and my hands begin to tremble. I stand up from table and look him in his eyes.

"I would sooner live on streets," I say, "than with one who disrespects me."

"Fine," he says. "Whatever."

I gather all my possessions (left shoe and right shoe) and march right down the stairs. When I open front door, I can see that the sky has turned gray and the clouds are beginning to drip. I do not care, though. I cannot stay inside another moment. I am about to step through door when I feel tiny hand gripping my elbow. It is Claire.

"Herschel, come on," she says. "Simon didn't mean all that. He's just hungover."

I point my finger at her face.

"Tell him that I hope his teeth fall out, except for one, so that he may get toothaches!"

"Herschel, come on. You don't mean that curse."

"I do," I say. "I mean curse."

I start to step through door, but she grabs me once again.

"Herschel, this is ridiculous!" she says. "You don't know anybody in Brooklyn, or where anything is, or how anything works."

I reach into pocket and take out my seven Indian pennies.

"I have seven cents more than when I first came to this land. I have started from scratch here before. I can start here from scratch once again."

"Herschel, trust me, you'll never make it."

I would never violence a woman. But when she says these words, I feel the urge to do so.

"Do you know who you are speaking with?" I say, my voice like the growl of an animal. "I am Herschel Rich!"

She swallows. The rain is pouring down now and I must shout to be heard.

"I crossed an ocean without pants!" I remind her. "I am not going to lie down in coffin! I am going to climb up this city until I have conquered my dream!"

I point at the brownstone down the block, the one Simon told me is for sale.

"How much is that building costing?"

"I don't know, Herschel. Probably, like, two million dollars."

"Tell Simon that I will earn the two millions first—and buy the big house before he can! And I will start new line of descendants *without* him. I may be old man of twenty-seven. But there is still grease in my bucket. There is still plenty of grease."

I put the seven pennies back in pocket and walk on through the rain. In the distance, I can see the Statue of Liberty. I figure that is as good a direction as any. I button my wool and march forward.

Even though I possess seven pennies, I know I must be careful about spending them. New York is expensive city. There is no telling how long they will last.

The trick to surviving with low funds is to not have such high standards. For example, in Slupsk, you could buy bowl of milk for three rubles. But they would sell you milk for just two rubles if you drank it directly from goat. It was not easy drinking from the goat, because she was strong and had problems with her anger. Still, a ruble is a ruble, and I always made sure to refuse bowl. As the saying goes in Slupsk: "Sometimes you must drink milk right out of the goat, because it costs two rubles instead of the three rubles."

I think about this saying as I walk the streets of Brooklyn. There are so many decadent restaurants, each one more luxurious than the last. I pass one named in honor of the pirate Long John Silver, which serves assorted treasures from the sea. Then I pass one that serves chicken that is crisped, in the style of Kentucky. Most amazing to me is a large white castle that sells Salisbury steaks between breads. Their food is so rich I can smell it from the street. My stomach is rumbling, but I know that these places are beyond me. Their signs are spelled out with electric flashing lights. If I want to survive, I must find someplace more humble.

Eventually, after hours of walking, I find simple market. I can tell from its bare green sign and drab brick walls that it is modest and affordable. I take out my pennies and go inside, grateful to have come across this "Whole Foods."

I select my potato and wait in line to buy. It is on the small side but very clean, without any filth on its skin. I am very excited to eat it.

A woman in man's clothes calls me over to her cash register.

"Will you need a bag?" she asks as I hand her my meal.

"No," I say. "I have pocket."

"That's the spirit!" she says. "I wish everyone were as eco as you."

"Is fine," I say. I am very hungry and want her to hurry with her movements. Eventually, she sets down my potato and weighs it. Then she looks at her screen and tells me the price.

I do not remember losing consciousness, but I am able now to piece together events. First I hear price of potato. Then I begin to shake. My vision blurs and I hear sound of screaming. After long time, I realize that it is my own voice. I am the one who is screaming. I fall on ground and lose some time. When I wake up, the woman is kneeling over me.

"Sir," she says, "would you like us to call someone?"

I glare at her. By this point, my shock has turned to rage.

"I want you to call the police," I say. "And arrest yourself for *robbery*."

I point my finger at her face.

"How can you sleep at night charging eight dimes for potato from the ground? You are so greedy, so evil—like a monster!"

I gesture wide with my arms.

"This store is run by monsters!"

At this point, something strange happens, which is that the other customers in the Whole Foods start applauding. I am very confused. I decide it is best idea to flee.

I run through a door in the back and find myself in area with trash. I am catching my breath when I hear the sound of laughter.

"Whoa," a young man says. "Score."

I look and see a gang of bearded hobos. They are scavenging through trash bin, picking out packages of food.

"Check the sell-by date," one says. "I bet these things aren't even stale."

It is amazing, I think, that these bums have so happy a spirit. I decide it is safe to introduce myself. I step out of the shadows and hold up my palms in show of peace.

"I am Herschel," I say. "From village of Slupsk."

"Cool," one of them says. "An international student."

Another one squints at my wool and pokes his fingers at the buttons.

"Where'd you get this?" he asks. "Housing Works?"

"I make it from old rags," I admit.

For some reason, this pathetic fact impresses them.

"That's rad," they say. "Talk about DIY."

"I am very hungry," I say.

"You came to the right place," says the man with the longest beard. "We've been Dumpster diving all semester, and this place is by far the sickest."

I do not want to become sick, but my hunger is extreme. I say a quick prayer and then dive inside the trash bin.

"Oh my God," I say when my eyes adjust to the light. "There is so much food!"

"I know," says the long-beard man. "Have you ever seen anything so fucking First World? It's, like, 'Hey, I've got a good idea. Let's rape the earth with chemicals, wrap the crops in plastic, drive them across the country, then bury them all in a landfill.'"

"Is fine," I say. I am not really listening. There are so many foods in front of me that my mouth has started dripping. Suddenly, I see something shocking. There is entire package of beef sausage completely unopened. Somehow the hobos have missed the best item. I rip off the wrapper and shove it in my face before anyone can take it from me. The meat is so delicious that my eyes fill up with tears. When I climb out of Dumpster, the bums are all staring at me, a look of horror in their eyes.

"I am sorry," I say, offering them rest of my sausage. "We can share the remaining flesh."

They hop back a step, like they are afraid.

"We're freegans," one of them says.

"Where is Freega?" I ask them.

"It's a political philosophy," the long-beard man explains. "We only eat discarded food that's cruelty-free."

"Why?" I ask.

They all start speaking rapidly of books and essays they have read. Their words are so long I cannot understand how they have learned them. Eventually, though, I understand their point: their parents are millionaires and they live this way for sport. I am so impressed, I nearly drop my sausage.

"Someday I will be wealthy like you," I vow. "And you will teach me to play your rich-man games."

I lean back into Dumpster and grab more meats. Soon, I have stuffed my coat so full that one of my pockets unravels. A penny falls out and I watch with panic as it rolls toward the group of wealthy children. A boy with glasses picks it up and gasps.

"Whoa," he says. "How did you get this?"

"Through labors," I say. "Please return."

"It's a 1906," he says, squinting at the coin. "And barely circulated. Holy shit—look at the polish on that Indian head!"

His bearded comrade glares at him.

"*Indian* head?"

"Sorry," the boy says. "First Nation...head."

He clears his throat and smiles at me.

"How much do you want for this thing?"

At this point, I begin to get excited. I do not know much of coins, but I am skillful with negotiations.

"How much will you pay?" I ask.

The boy reaches into his pocket and pulls out clump of moneys.

"I'll give you ten bucks."

I bite my lip to keep myself from grinning. Ten dollars is more than one week's salary in pickle factory. I want to take his offer, but I know I must hold out for more. When there is an opportunity in life, you must take biggest advantage.

"Twelve," I say, speaking firmly.

A long time passes. My heart is beating so fast in my chest, I am worried the freegans can hear it.

"Fine," says the boy with the glasses. "Twelve."

He peels me off some banknotes and chuckles to himself.

"Where else am I gonna find another 1906, right?"

I smile with triumph and pull out rest of pennies.

"Right here," I say—and sell them all.

I spend the afternoon by water, eating my sausage and counting my stack of moneys. It is eighty-four dollars, more than I have seen in my whole life. I know from experience in Whole Foods that prices in Brooklyn have increased. But it is still a sizable fortune — enough to buy more potatoes than I could even carry.

As I gaze at the Statue of Liberty, I begin to think of Sarah. Sometimes, when it was too cold to sleep, she would ask me to speak make-believe.

"Close your eyes," I would say as I wrapped blanket tight around her body. "I have found gold on the street and we are rich."

Then I would tell story of our day. For breakfast we eat entire tin of herring. Then we take bath, using water so hot it can melt soap. In the middle of work, we take hour-long break from our factories. And what do we eat? Another tin of herring, our second of the day. It is even bigger than the first. We have seltzer from the cart. Each one of us gets our own glass. Would you like a refill? asks the seltzer man. Yes, I say, but please this time with flavors. I will have to charge double, he says. That is acceptable, I reply, the price does not upset me. We drink two more glasses of seltzer, with red and purple.

After work we meet and it is light, because we only labored for twelve hours. We put on store-bought clothes and spend the evening promenading. Sarah is dressed in ribbons that I have purchased new. She is so beautiful that no one can believe it. The women compliment her ribbons and her face, which is covered in the powder that she likes. I take her to the picture show and we sit in the cushioned chairs in front. You cannot sit there, says the usher, unless you order candied orange. That is not a problem, I say. Here is the money for candied orange. The man is shocked and has no choice but to bring us the candied orange in front of everyone. People see that he was wrong to doubt us.

For dinner we eat two more tins of herring. We are so full of foods, we do not even want to eat more. If there was more food there, we would not eat it. I crank the Victrola, which I have purchased in full, and we dance to the song of our choice. Then we lie with each other, on pillows stitched from cotton and stuffed with the feathers of a bird.

We always said that if I died in factory, or she from birthing child, then the other would keep fighting for this dream. It is one thing saying words, but another thing to live them.

I look out at the statue and imagine she is Sarah, dressed in stylish green robe from the Gimbels. With one arm she holds English book, which she used to teach me spell. With other arm, she waves to me from across the sparkling bay, her hand raised high in the clouds.

"Look, I found the money," I whisper to her. "It is just like how we dreamed."

She looks down on me with tight-pressed lips and steely eyes. I laugh to myself, because of course I have seen this expression before. It is like the look she gave me on her birthday, when I dipped into savings jar to buy her salted shrimps.

"Do not worry, my love," I say to her. "Your Herschel is not getting lazy."

I gaze into her bright-green eyes and grin.

"He is only just now getting started."

★   ★   ★

There are three important keys to pickling: patience, hard work, and rage. Rage, of these three, is by far the most vital. Pickling can be torture, like living inside endless nightmare. The only way to have success is to approach each day with violence.

As crazy as it is to believe, my eighty-four-dollar fortune is not so vast. Prices have changed in past one hundred years, and I must use my moneys cleverly.

I spend forty-two dollars on supplies I need to make first batch of pickles. That includes twenty glass jars, one tub of vinegar, garlic, salt, and herbs. I also buy ladle, to scoop water out from river. The cucumbers I get from the Whole Foods, inside their garbage bins.

It takes three days for scum to form in jars and pickles to be sour. During this time, I prepare my vending cart. It is not so hard because people in Cobble Hill are insane and leave perfect, clean furniture on sidewalk. I find dark-wood bureau outside of brownstone and place it on wheels of old baby carriage.

With rest of my money I buy living supplies, to help me survive until wealthy. For shelter, I buy tarp and rope at hardware store. For hygiene, I buy soap and toothbrush from Duane Reade. For eating, I go to Key Food and buy butter made from peanuts. All of these things together cost twenty-one dollars.

I also buy lockbox to keep all my money and crowbar in case there is thief, and I must violence. These two necessities cost me nineteen dollars.

I am left now with two dollars. If it runs out, I know I will have many troubles. But all I can feel is excitement. I know it sounds strange, but I have truly missed doing work.

When I was the rat man at pickle factory, I did not have

much influence on company policy. This was unfortunate, because sometimes I had decent ideas. For example, one day I realized that things would run better if the labeling girls wore hairnets, because they would not get pulled into the gears so much by their hair. I told my supervisor, and he nodded like he was listening, but the girls never got any hairnets and they kept getting pulled into the gears, about three of them each month, screaming, "No, my God!" while everybody wept and so on. It slowed production. I always dreamed someday I would be boss and run things in the way that I thought best.

Now that I have my own business, I am in charge of everything. I get to decide recipe (salt and garlics). I get to decide uniform (gray). I even get to decide name of company. It takes me long time to invent one, because titles are so important. It must be something snappy and stylish that will stick in people's heads. Eventually, after several hours, I think of good one and write it onto cart: SARAH'S STATUE OF LIBERTY GARLIC PICKLES WITH SALT PICKLE COMPANY.

All that is left to decide now is location—and it is easy choice.

I have spent ten days lounging on the western shore of Brooklyn, idling among the brownstones of the wealthy. But, if I am to succeed as peddler, I must go back to old neighborhood, where the streets are always clogged with hungry laborers. I must return at once to Williamsburg.

"Are these gluten-free?" the tattooed man asks me, holding up jar to his face.

I hesitate with fear. I have been at Driggs and Ninth since sunrise and he is first person I have seen.

"They are pickles," I explain.

He squints some more at jar.

"What about sulfites?" he asks.

I do not know his words, but I sense he is starting to lose interest. I decide it is good time to make pitch.

"Whole Foods sells pickle jar for seven. I sell for four and include all the scum."

I point to the scum, which has collected nicely inside top of jar. The man smiles tightly as he hands me back the pickles.

"I'll come back later," he says.

I sigh as he rides off on bicycle. It is almost seven and still I have no sales.

"Pickles here!" I scream. "Pickles with garlic and scum!"

My voice becomes hoarse, but still nobody comes. I do not understand it. The streets are mostly empty, even though the sun has risen. How could the people of Williamsburg sleep so late on a Thursday? Do they not have factories to go to? There must be some holiday that I do not know about.

I am thinking about finding new location, when I spot two skinny men eyeballing cart.

"Check it out," one of them says. "Artisanal pickles."

I stare at the pair. One has taken tiny gadget out of pocket.

"He's not on Yelp," he says. He picks up one of my pickle jars and holds it to the light.

"How local is your produce?" asks the other.

I am confused as usual but decide it is best not to show it.

"I make pickles here," I say. "In Brooklyn."

The men smile and nod, impressed for some reason by this information.

"And is it all natural?" one asks.

"What are you talking about?"

"Do you add any chemicals? Like benzoates or preservatives?"

"I do not know what any of that is."

The men nod some more, impressed again.

"You know what?" one of them says. "I think I'll take a jar."

He pulls out his wallet.

"Do you take Amex?"

"Only cash," I say.

"Good for you," he says. "The credit-card conglomerates are murdering small businesses. If we're going to fight them, we need to start on the microlevel."

"Is fine," I say. "Four dollars."

I crack my neck and get into haggling stance. But, to my shock, he does not argue price.

"Here you go," he says, taking dollars from his pocket. I grab them and stuff them into lockbox before he can change his mind.

When I look up, the men have opened the pickle jar and are sniffing the brine.

"It's got an amazing bouquet," one says with his eyes closed tight. "Really vegetal."

"It'll go great with the quinoa," says the other.

After some more strange sniffs, they close the jar and start to walk away. They are holding hands, I notice. I am so confused by this that I almost forget to shout important thing.

"Wait!" I call out after them. "You must bring back jar!"

They turn around and squint at me.

"Excuse me?"

"You must bring it back when you are done," I explain. "So that I can reuse."

"You reclaim your jars?"

"There is nothing wrong with reusing jars," I say. "You can fill them again and again and taste is same."

"Amen to that," the man says.

"You must return jar," I repeat firmly. "Or I will violence."

The man rubs his chin and then smiles.

"You know what?" he says. "I think I'm going to write a blog post about you."

"A what?"

"A blog post."

"A what?"

"A post. On my blog."

"A what?"

"A blog post."

"Fine," I say. "Is fine."

WilliamsburgFoodie.com

No label. No logo. No website. Just pure, authentic taste.

My discovery of the perfect pickle, by Chris LeBoz

We've seen so many touted picklers crash and burn this season—La Pickle, Cuke, Das Pickle. So I was fairly skeptical when I came across this cart (see photos after jump). How could I be sure I wasn't falling for another gimmick? How could I be sure these pickles were authentic?

One sniff of brine erased my cynicism. The fact of the matter is, if you haven't had Sarah's Statue of Liberty Garlic Pickles with Salt, you haven't had a real pickle.

Herschel Rich handcrafts his artisanal pickles locally, using freegan cucumbers, unpasteurized river water, and reclaimed glass jars. The pungent taste is not for everyone. And the floating salt scum takes some getting used to. But guess what? *This is what pickles are supposed to taste like.* If it's too much for you to handle, head to Walmart, I guess, and buy yourself some jumbo Vlasics.

Herschel doesn't water down his pickles—or his politics. He refuses to use chemical additives, relying entirely on all-natural, locavore ingredients. In fact, his devotion to conservation is so extreme, he *personally reclaims his pickle jars from customers.* When I asked him to explain this unusual practice, he clenched his fists with passion.

"There is nothing wrong with reusing jars," he said. "You must return jar."

In a land of DIY pretenders, Herschel is, quite simply, the "real deal." His cart is constructed entirely of salvaged wood. His clothing is homemade from repurposed rags. And his product name seems

purposefully designed to be as noncommercial as
possible.

So head to Williamsburg this afternoon. Your taste
buds (and conscience) will thank you.

Next day I sell out batch in fifteen minutes. The people are coming at me so fast I cannot believe it. They are like animals,
crazed for these pickles! It is like time in Slupsk that there was
plague and only one witch selling medicine.

When I am down to last jar, there are still many people in
line. Two people rush to cart and begin screaming.

"I was here first," says bald man with black glasses. "I've
been waiting here since seven."

"That's not true," says tiny Chinawoman. She has ring in
nose like pig.

There is lots of arguing back and forth.

"Look," says the bald man finally, "I wasn't going to say anything. But I work for Jake Gyllenhaal."

At this point, I am frightened. I have not heard of this Jake
man, but I can tell from crowd's reaction he is probably sheriff
or constable.

"I am sorry," I say to woman. "I must do as I am told."

"That's bullshit!" she screams.

"I am sorry," I repeat.

I am handing the jar to the man when the Chinawoman
pokes me on the shoulder.

"I'll give you five dollars!" she shouts.

I stop my movements.

"Oh my God," I say. It is first time in life I have seen price go up in a market. I have never been this shocked, including the time I was brined a hundred years.

"Oh my God," I say again. "My God."

I am about to hand woman the jar when the man shouts, "Six dollars!"

At this point, something strange happens, which is that my body begins to dance. I am trying to be professional and keep my face normal, but my legs and arms have all begun to dance.

"Seven!"

"Eight!"

"Nine!"

The man reaches into his pocket, pulls out his wallet, and counts all the bills inside.

"Seventeen!"

I assume this must be the end, but then the woman pulls out twenty-dollar bill. It is like I am in strange dream. What are all these millionaires doing in Williamsburg?

I take the Chinawoman's money and stand on cart to address the growing crowd.

"I am out of pickles," I say, causing everyone to groan. "But do not be afraid! I will return in three days with giant batch."

The people begin to cheer, like I am Elijah announcing the Messiah.

"Also," I add softly, "I am going to raise prices."

From that point on, I sell jars for twelve dollars. You would think this outrageous figure would slow sales, but it is the opposite. The more I charge, the more people want the pickles. By end of second week, I have $2,219 in lockbox.

I am happy to be making such big profits. But secretly part of me wishes people haggled. Screaming over money is what makes the market fun. Sarah used to threaten to kill the potato man whenever his prices went up. She would take out her knife and say, "I will kill you with this knife for robbing me." He would curse her in Hungarian and then the two of them would wave their fists around. It was good times for everyone. These days, though, nobody has that kind of will. It is all please and thank you and have a nice day.

One evening I am selling jar when I hear familiar voices. I look across street. It is Claire and Simon. She is pulling him toward me by the wrist while he struggles to break free.

"I don't want to," he is whispering, like toddler being dragged to work his loom. *"No."*

Eventually, he manages to flee her and darts into the Starbucks Café. Claire sighs and continues toward my pickle cart.

"Herschel!" she shouts. "Over here!"

"I am with customer," I tell her. I complete my sale, lock money into box, and only then turn toward her.

"Hello," I say.

She gestures at my money cart and laughs.

"This is so cool!" she says. "Herschel, your cart looks *amazing.*"

"Is fine," I say with modesty.

"Simon and I were reading *New York Magazine*," she says, "and we saw your cart in the Approval Matrix. We couldn't believe it!"

"I am in magazine?"

"Herschel, you're everywhere!" she says. *"Gawker, Eater, Brooklyn Vegan.* You're a huge success!"

"I am nowhere close to success," I tell her. "I vowed I would buy house for two millions. I have barely made two thousands."

"That's pretty good for two weeks," she says.

"Is nothing," I tell her. "Like pennies compared to what is coming."

She laughs out loud, as if I am making joke.

"You are not the first to doubt me," I tell her. "When I was saving wages to leave Slupsk, my father told me that I dream too big. He urged me to stay and join his business."

"What did he do?"

"He was shit collector."

Claire scrunches up her face.

"What's that?"

"What do you think it is? It is person who collects shit. He owned big shit cart, and every day he went around collecting shit. He smelled like shit and was always covered in shit. Finally, after many years with the shit, he saved money up for house. But before he could even go inside, the Cossacks got drunk and burned it. All that was saved was his shit cart, which the Cossacks had shit inside."

"Wow," she says. "You must hate those Cossacks."

"No," I say. "I am thankful to them. They gave me the rage I needed to work harder than most men."

Claire nods.

"I can see where Simon gets his work ethic from."

I raise my eyebrows.

"Simon has work ethic?"

"Sure," she says. "I mean... it's less extreme now than when he was first starting out in the business. But he still really pushes himself. Like, last week, a studio asked him to write some movie taglines? And his allergies were acting up. So I was, like, 'Just tell them you're sick.' But he sat down and wrote them anyway."

"That sounds like real struggle," I say, winking hard to show I am being facetious.

I look across the street. Simon has still not left the café. There is nothing to do but make more conversation with Claire.

"How is your schooling?" I ask.

"Just trying to figure out my dissertation," she says. "It's hard to pick a topic. There are so many aspects of the immigration process in need of reform."

I wave my hands.

"Is fine," I say.

"How can you say that? You went through hell to make it to this country."

"Jews do not believe in hell," I remind her. "That is strange Christian thing. But also, more important, I think you spend too much time thinking of others."

She smiles. "What a nice thing to say."

"I meant it as insult. In Slupsk we have popular saying. It goes: 'You must always put yourself first, before everybody else, in every situation in the world, even if you have resources and they are about to die.'"

"That's a little harsh."

"Is necessary. You have just one life. If you give it to another, it is gone."

Claire looks across the street. Simon is hiding behind lamppost, slurping coffee frosting drink. She waves at him, and he reluctantly approaches us.

"Hello," I say when we are face-to-face.

"Hey," he says.

Claire takes out her pocket phone and smiles.

"I have to make a call."

"That is lie!" I say. She ignores me and crosses the street, leaving me with my great-great-grandson.

Simon is twenty-seven, just like me. But sometimes it is hard to believe he is that old. His posture is terrible, so although we are same height, I am always looking down on him, like he is boy.

I also have trouble believing he is wealthy. I know he has made moneys, because this is basically all he ever speaks of. But his hygiene is so terrible he resembles newsboy. His breath is so awful from his coffees, it is torture to stand near him. His hair is full of dandruffs, his ears are filled with wax, and his teeth are stained like monster from the picture show. My standard for cleanliness is not so high. My father, as you recall, was shit collector. So when I say man needs to clean himself, it is pretty big statement.

Simon crouches next to my sign and laughs.

"Twelve dollars a *jar?*" he says. "Holy shit. People don't actually pay that, do they?"

"I have had hundreds of customers," I inform him.

"They must have been tourists or something."

"They were New Yorkers," I say. "They came because my pickles were inside their *New York Magazine*."

"You were in *New York*?" Simon says. "Huh. Don't know how I missed that. Was it a long article?"

"It was in Approval Matrix, and I know that you have seen it because Claire told me you have seen it! You lie to pretend you are not jealous, but really you are jealous!"

Simon turns red and is silent for long time. Eventually, he picks up jar and squints at it.

"No labels, huh?"

"They are unnecessary expense."

"I wonder if the Health Department thinks so."

He grins at me, his yellow teeth moist like a dog's.

"Maybe I'll pay them a visit?" he says.

At this point I am hungering to violence him. I take long, slow breath to calm myself.

"If you pay them a visit," I warn him, "you will soon get two more visits. The first will be from my fists. And the second will be from Malakh HaMavet, the Angel of Death."

We do not speak until Claire has returned.

"Well?" she says brightly. "What did I miss?"

"Nothing," Simon mutters. "Come on."

He flags a yellow taxi car and drags her inside the backseat.

"Bye, Herschel!" Claire cries through the window. "Good luck!"

I shout as loud as possible, so Simon can hear my words.

"I do not need lucks! I do not need *anything!*"

*   *   *

The home I made with Sarah was very pleasant, but it did have several flaws. For example, the stove often caught fire, there was no indoor bathroom, and we shared our room with fifteen other Jews.

Sarah and I slept in mattress in the corner, behind curtains stitched from flour sacks. The curtains took us many days to sew, but we worked fast and hard (we had just been wed and needed privacy for married acts).

Since moving from Simon's couch, I have been sleeping in McCarren Park. It is not so bad. I bathe in public toilet and tie tarp to tree for shelter. Sometimes the policemen come with lights and chase me, but I am quick and not afraid of them.

I have $4,128 and could easily buy my way into some household. But it would be needless expenditure. I have trained my body to sleep just four hours each night, since that is all the body really needs, and why should I care where I spend such small portion of the day? I am comfortable on my own and do not miss having companions around. Being alone is nothing for me. Is fine.

One night, though, while lying under tarp behind toilet, I realize something: in order to increase pickle production, I must have more storage space for jars. I can only fit fifty in cart, plus four in coat and two in pants. In order to expand my business, it is vital to find myself a room.

The cheapest one I find is out in Bushwick. According to flyer, rent is four hundred dollars per month. When I show up at building, there is line of young people gathered on street. A short man with green hair addresses them.

"Please have your portfolios ready," he says. "Thank you!"

"What is this place?" I ask young girl holding stack of strange photographs.

"It's called the Vortex Factory," she says. "It's the most selective artist colony east of Williamsburg."

I do not understand most of her words, but I am happy to hear it is factory. I have always gotten along with fellow laborers.

Eventually, after waiting long time, I am motioned inside by green-haired man. When I step through the door, I gasp. The space is gigantic, big enough to house at least ten thousand pickle jars.

"Oh my God," I say.

"I know," he says. "It's pretty incredible."

One area is covered in tarps and splattered with paint. Another is crowded with drums and electric pianos. I cannot see where they are making their vortexes.

There are many sleeping peoples on the floor, huddled on mattresses, surrounded by empty alcohols. There are lagers, wines, spirits—more bottles than I have ever seen.

"Was their wedding last night?" I ask.

The green-haired man laughs. He does not answer my question about wedding.

"Come on," he says. "I'll show you around."

He walks me through factory, telling me names of sleeping boarders.

"That's Jordan," he says, pointing to man with beard. "He's an experimental poet."

"I have not heard of him," I admit.

"You will," he says. "His stuff's incredible. He just got his MFA."

I do not know what is this "MFA," but it must be rare achievement, because when he says it his eyebrows go up.

"Who is she?" I ask, pointing to snoring woman.

"That's Alison," he says. "She's an actress."

I squint at the woman. She is homely and overweight with many blemishes on face.

"*Radio* actress?" I ask.

"Spoken word, mostly," he says. "She just got her MFA. She's incredible."

He points to group of hairy, filthy men.

"Those guys just got their MFAs," he tells me. "In painting, sculpture, and sound design. They're in a noise band called the Fuzz."

"I have not heard of them, either," I admit.

"You will," he says. "Their music's just . . ."

He pauses, thinking of way to describe.

"It's incredible," he says.

He folds his arms and smiles at me.

"So. Let's have a look at your portfolio."

My face flushes.

"I do not know what that means."

He laughs.

"You know what? Me neither. The idea that art belongs in a manila folder—it's preposterous. The here and now is where the truth's alive. The moment you try to document it, the immediacy is lost."

"Is fine," I say, confused.

"So tell me, what would you bring to the Vortex Factory?"

"Just myself," I say. "And many jars of pickles."

He rubs his chin and squints at me.

"So you work in installations?"

"I sell pickles from cart," I explain. "First I make salt brine, then I put in cucumbers, then I wheel cart and shout out, 'Pickles, pickles!'"

"So there's a pretty big performance element to your art."

At this point I am starting to get frustrated.

"It is not performance," I say. "It is my life. It is what I must do to survive."

He smiles at me with look of admiration.

"Dude," he says, "that's incredible."

I get biggest room in the whole house.

"How's it going?" Claire asks me the next day at my cart.

"I am working," I tell her. "I have no time to socialize."

Her pants are so tight I cannot even believe it. I can see the shape of her kneecaps. It is crazy to me that she can dress this way and not be thrown in jail.

"There's nobody in line," she says.

I look. Is true.

"Still, somebody might come," I say. "I only have time to speak with customers."

"Okay, fine," she says. "In that case, I'll take a jar."

"Twelve dollars."

She folds her arms and smirks at me.

"I'll give you four bucks."

My eyes widen. I was not expecting this.

"Twelve dollars," I say firmly. "That is price."

"That's outrageous," she says. "I'll give you six and you'll be lucky to get it."

"Ten dollars," I say. "And you can choose which jar."

"The jars are all the same," she says. "I'll give you seven and that's final."

"It must be ten."

"It must be seven."

"Nine!" I shout.

"Eight!" she screams.

"Fine!" I say.

She laughs. I must admit, part of me is impressed.

She takes out her dollars and I pluck them from her hand, careful not to touch her ungloved fingers.

"Now can you take a break?" she asks.

"Is fine," I say, after some thought.

We walk to curb across the street, so I can keep eyes on cart. She asks me where I am living and I tell her about Vortex Factory.

"Wow," she says. "You're turning into a real hipster."

I do not know this word, so I just nod.

"It is good you are here," I tell her.

She smiles at me.

"How come?"

"Because you must deliver this to Simon."

I reach into coat and pull out wad of bills.

"It is a hundred and thirty dollars," I tell her. "I calculate one week's rent inside his house, plus the cost of board."

She opens her mouth like she is going to argue, but I silence her with look of major violence.

"Okay, okay," she says. "I'll give it to him the next time I see him."

"When will that be?" I ask. I am eager for my debt to be settled.

"I don't know," she says. "We're kind of in a fight right now."

"About what? Has he beaten you?"

"No, nothing like that. He's just been impossible lately. He won't let me throw an ACLU fund-raiser at his house. He says he cares about politics, but I don't even think he's registered to vote."

She looks at my cart and reads out loud the name I have on sign.

"Sarah was my wife," I explain. "I name business after her."

She nods her head slowly.

"You must really miss her."

"Is fine," I say. "There is nothing to do about it."

"What was she like?" she asks.

I shrug.

"I do not know how to describe her."

"Is the pickle recipe hers?"

I shake my head.

"She did not waste time on pickles," I say. "She was real cook. She made tzimmes, latkes, cabbage soups with schmaltz..."

I begin to see her in my mind, her curly brown hair and the freckle on her cheek. I try to resume story but cannot for some reason. It is hard to catch my breath.

"She sounds wonderful," Claire says.

"She was good, strong help," I say.

I clear my throat and stand up.

"Of course, she would not appreciate us talking for so long."
She grins.

"Why not?"

"Because she did not like me taking breaks."

As I am heading back to pickle cart, I look over shoulder.

"You must come back sometime!" I shout at her.

"Oh yeah?" she says.

"Of course. Every customer must return jar."

I do not spend much time with my six roommates, because they keep strange hours. When I leave with cart at 4:00 a.m., they have all just gone to sleep. And when I return from work, at 10:00 p.m., they are out for nightly celebration.

I do not know what it is they celebrate. In all my time in Vortex Factory, I have yet to see them sell a single vortex, or anything else for that matter. I assume that just before I joined their house, they have had some major group success. It is only explanation for their joy.

I am not opposed to celebrations. In fact, I have been planning one for weeks. After selling my first batch of pickles, I went to Key Food and bought tin of herring. It cost me seven dollars — more than double peanut butter — but I purchased anyway. I said to myself, *When I have ten thousands saved up, I will reward my body with this tasty fish.*

By end of my first month in the Vortex, I am selling fifty jars a day. I learn to stagger batches in my closet, so there are always pickles that are ready. I am making six hundred dollars each shift, over three thousand dollars each week. One morning I count savings and I cannot believe it: I have nine thousand seven hundred twenty-seven dollars. That night, before sleep, I put special tin of herring in my coat. By lunch break, I hope, I will have the occasion to eat it.

I am setting up cart the next day when I hear my name spoken. I turn toward the voice and see Negro woman wearing man's suit and holding clipboard.

"I'm Kalisha Sanders," she says to me. "I'd like to ask you a few questions."

"The pickles have no glutens," I recite. "The vegetables are freegan and the water is all locavore."

"And do you have a vendor's license?"

"A what?"

"A license," she says. "For running a food cart."

I try to make words, but I cannot. I am caught completely by surprise.

"I'm from the Department of Health," says the Kalisha. "And I've had some complaints about your operation."

My fists clench with fury.

"Who was the informer? Was it Simon Rich?"

She ignores me and picks up jar of pickles.

"Whoa," she says. "Is that scum?"

"Is all-natural," I murmur.

"You're lucky there hasn't been an E. coli outbreak."

She takes out stack of papers and hands it to me.

"Here's a summary of your violations. Vending without a license in a nonvending zone is one thousand two hundred and fifty dollars. The health-code fines, altogether, come to two thousand seven hundred dollars."

"Oh my God," I say. "My God."

She glances at my box of cash and sighs.

"I assume you haven't declared any of your earnings for tax purposes."

"Tax what?"

She hands me another form.

"Send this in with your payment to the city treasury," she says. "And get this cart off the street. I don't want to see you out here until you're fully compliant."

By the time I can make myself speak, she has started to walk away.

"Stop!" I say. "Wait. Let us talk about this."

She turns around and squints at me.

"What is there to talk about?"

I take deep, slow breath to steady self. I have been in this situation before. I was leaving Slupsk when Cossacks asked me to pay them "nighttime road tax." I gave them all vodkas and they let me through. The trick in these matters is to handle things delicately, with smooth words and manner.

"Here is bribe," I say, throwing twenty-dollar bill at her. "Take it, please, and go."

Her eyes widen and she takes step toward me.

"Did you just say what I think you said?"

I clear my throat. She is very good haggler, and I am impressed.

"*Thirty*-dollar bribe," I say. "Plus one free pickle jar each week."

"Unbelievable," she says.

She scribbles note on clipboard and then glares at me.

"Pay those fines quick," she tells me. "Or I'll shut you down for good."

By the time I cart pickles back to Vortex Factory, my roommates are awake.

"Herschel's in the house!" says the green-haired man. "Where've you been, killer?"

"I have been working," I tell him, my voice low with misery. "But now I can work no more."

"Cool," the actress says. "Then you can get mimosas with us."

"Thank you for invitation," I say, "but today I have nothing to celebrate."

I lock myself in room and put herring back in drawer. Then I lay the government documents on mattress. I understand parts of the forms, like "Name" and "Address." But the rest confuses me and makes my head hurt.

I have dealt with American authorities before, when coming to Ellis Island. They made me wait in line for nineteen hours, then flipped up my eyelids and shoved wooden sticks into my eyeballs. It was not great, but I would take it over this "W-2."

It is almost nightfall when I hear knock on my door.

"Wassup, Hersch," says the green-haired man. He is drunk from celebrations.

"Wassup to you as well," I say politely.

"Some girl's here to see you," he tells me, his lips curled into giant grin.

I sigh. It is probably inspector to arrest me. I am thinking of fleeing through window, when I look into the hallway and catch sight of yellow hair.

"Claire?" I say. "What are you doing here?"

She holds up empty pickle jar.

"Just returning this," she says. "You weren't at your usual spot."

She passes me jar, which she has cleaned with soaps.

"You can keep it," I say.

I mean for my voice to sound formal, but it comes out soft and broken. I have vowed to the world that I will be success, but setbacks have transformed me into liar. My stomach is sick with shame.

"Is everything okay?" Claire asks.

"Is fine," I say.

She notices my legal forms, picks them up, and whistles.

"Whoa," she says. "Herschel, you got *nailed*."

She flips through them one at a time, shaking her head back and forth.

"These vendor forms are unconscionable," she says. "Even a native English-speaker would have problems understanding them. The entire system's completely prejudicial against immigrants."

I nod in agreement.

"It was very confusing when the Negress refused my bribe."

Claire coughs.

"Herschel," she says, putting hand onto my shoulder, "I think you should consider letting me help you with your business."

I shake her off.

"I am not one who takes charity."

"Everyone needs help sometimes."

"Not me," I say. "Is fine. I will figure out forms on my own."

Claire folds her arms. "What's your Social Security number?"

"Social what?"

She starts to unzip her pack. I sit on bed and sigh. It is too late now to stop her.

"Don't worry," she says. "It's going to be okay."

She reaches into bag and smiles.

"I've got my lucky troll."

Claire hands me her computer box and points at grid of numbers.

"There!" she says. "I made you a spreadsheet. This number's all your fines, this number's all your tax obligations, and this number's the investments you'll have to make in order to become health-code compliant."

"What is this red number? With minus sign in front of it?"

She hesitates.

"Your profits."

I begin to feel dizzy. We have been working several hours without an interruption, and now I can no longer run from truth.

"The business has failed," I admit to Claire. "There is no way for it to make moneys."

"That's not true," she says. "You could increase production."

I shake my head.

"Impossible. I am already filling cart up to brim with jars, and also my coat and pants."

"Then you'll need to get some workers," she says, entering numbers into computer. "If you put six more carts on the street, you could easily net two thousand dollars every week."

I hesitate.

"Maybe is smart idea," I admit. "But workers cost."

"You could get interns."

I raise my eyebrows; this word is unfamiliar.

"'Interns'?"

It takes long time, but eventually she is able to explain this thing to me.

"So they are slaves," I say. "And it is not illegal?"

She hesitates.

"Basically."

She types business description onto Columbia University website. Within minutes, there are messages from students desiring to do my slave labor, all of it for free, in exchange for nothing.

"My God," I say, my heart speeding up. "My God!"

I leap up from bed, my hands trembling with excitement. I can feel my legs begin to dance.

"Lye dye dye!" I sing. "Lye, dye dye dye, dye dye!"

I dance for some time.

"Claire!" I say when I have caught my breath. "You have saved me!"

"It was nothing," she says. "A piece of the cake, right?"

I take her hand and squeeze, even though she has no glove.

"You are good, strong help," I say.

She bites her lip, her cheeks turning bright red.

"Okay, enough resting," I tell her. "It is time to return to work."

You cannot murder interns, but other than that, they are the same as mules. You can rob them, abuse them, debase them. There are no limits. When a man agrees to be intern, he is saying, "I am no longer human being with rights, I am like dog or monkey. Use me for labor until my body breaks and then consume all of my meats."

I would sooner die than serve as intern. But for students of Columbia University, it is very popular. Within one day, a hundred men and women send me résumés in the hope that I will choose them as my slaves.

"This girl looks impressive," Claire says, picking résumé out from giant stack. "She was editor of the *Spectator*. That's the big Columbia student paper."

"She is too fat," I say. "She will eat all of my pickles."

"Herschel, that's really insensitive," Claire says. "You know, it's illegal not to hire someone based on their looks."

"I am not hiring anyone," I remind her. "I am choosing interns."

Claire sighs. Part of her, I can tell, regrets having told me about concept of interns. But now it is too late. I know about interns and will always have interns, until the day I die.

"I want forty strong bucks," I command, "with large hands for carrying."

Claire pretends as if she does not hear me.

"How about this guy?" she says. "He's a computer-science major. I bet he'd design us a website."

"A what?"

"A site on the Web."

"A what?"

"A website."

I shrug.

"Is fine."

sarahsstatueoflibertygarlicpickleswithsaltpickle
company.com

"Herschel's Dream"

Press release by Graham Metzger, media-relations
intern

Herschel Rich came to this country with a bold
mission: to achieve success without compromising his
radical belief system. Now, after years of struggle,
his dream is becoming a reality.

Herschel's anticorporate commitment to agricul-
tural sustainability has won him accolades all over
this city. The New York Times called his pickles a
"hipster delicacy," and Lady Gaga tweeted that his
pickles "will make you see God." Jay Z recently
announced that Herschel's pickles will be the official pickles of the Brooklyn Nets, with their own
stand at the Barclays Center.

But no one appreciates Herschel more than the young men and women who work for him.

"Herschel changed my life," said Josh Herson, a rising junior at Columbia, who mans one of Herschel's forty pickle carts. "Last year at this time I was thinking about becoming a banker or working for some soulless ad firm. But interning for Herschel has shown me that you don't have to sell out to succeed."

According to Claire Whitman, the company's chief spokeswoman, pickles are only the beginning. Sarah's Statue of Liberty Garlic Pickles with Salt Pickle Company intends to open a political action center in Williamsburg, with a focus on immigration reform. And an art zine is being planned in collaboration with the Vortex Factory, the profits of which will be donated to worthy causes.

When I asked Herschel about these developments, he responded with the pithy poeticism that has made him such a cultural icon in Williamsburg.

"Everyone must return jar. Or they will be severely violenced."

It's hard to think of a better metaphor for our times. If we don't give back to society—if we don't "return our jars"—then our world may very well fall apart. Luckily, we have Herschel to help us hold it all together.

★　　★　　★

Strange things soon begin to happen. People start to camera me when I am manning cart. Customers ask me to write my name on jars that they have bought. One day, newspaper lady asks my opinion on "Occupy movement." I do not understand her words and so I let Claire answer.

"Our company believes in the value of all human beings," she says. "We stand for the ninety-nine percent."

She says many things like this to many people. Her words are crazy, but I do not stop her, because it is making more people buy our pickles. Every day, there are more and more customers lining up.

"This is so wonderful," she says to me one night while helping me count out the day's moneys.

"Yes," I say. "At this rate, I will soon be rich."

Claire laughs like I have made joke. She tells me she is taking leave of absence from her studies, to help me with company full-time. I am very surprised.

"Simon has allowed this?"

"I finally broke up with him," she says. "I just couldn't take it anymore. Every day I was with him, it was like I was losing a piece of my soul. I decided, if I'm going to invest in a relationship, I want it to be with somebody authentic. Somebody humble and principled. And real."

She looks into my eyes and smiles.

"You know what I mean, Herschel?"

I nod. I have not really been listening, because I was busy counting moneys, but she said my name, so I know it is my turn to speak.

"Yes," I say. "Is fine."

She reaches into lockbox and squeezes my hand. Eventually, she lets go, and I am able to go back to counting moneys.

One day, I am at my pickle stand—sorry, *one* of my pickle stands—when two men in black suits show up. They say they are from Walmart and are trying to connect with youth market. It is their hope that I will collaborate with them on a "multi-platform, Millennial-targeted marketing campaign."

I do not understand, and so, as usual, I let Claire speak.

"We're not interested," she says. "Please leave."

I nod with agreement; these men have bought no pickles and are holding up the line.

"If you do not want to buy jars," I say, "you must get out of here!"

The men in suits shrug and walk away. As soon as they are out of sight, my interns all applaud. I am confused.

"That was amazing!" Claire says as she throws her arms around me. "You totally blew off those corporate douche bags!"

"Is fine," I say.

In the distance, I see the Walmart men climb into large black car. It is very long, I notice, and also very shiny. I begin to grow curious about them.

"Who is this Walmart?" I ask Claire.

"They're one of the most evil corporations on earth," she says. "They exploit immigrants, sell poisonous junk food, and destroy small businesses. It's ridiculous. They think they can just show up here, write a check, and get whomever they want to do their bidding—"

I interrupt her.

"What is check?"

"It's, like, money."

I run so fast that both my shoes fall off. Eventually, after several blocks of screaming and waving my arms in the air, I catch up to these wonderful Walmart people. They open their door and I leap inside car before they have time to change their mind.

The deal is very fair. They give me two hundred thousand dollars, enough to make down payment on house that I need to defeat Simon. In exchange, I give them rights to my likeness, name, face, and identity, to use however they want, in unlimited ads, forever.

I also agree to sell pickle company to Walmart. Their plan is to rename it "Brooklyn Hipster Pickles" and replace all ingredients with chemicals.

"Is fine," I say.

In exchange for giving them company, I receive thirty thousand shares of their precious, beautiful stock, which is valued at $74.34 per share.

I announce my news the next day at the Vortex Factory. My roommates are still sleeping, because it is not yet noon, but Claire and my interns are all present. It takes me long time to describe the deal, because I cannot stop dancing. Eventually, though, after much dancing, I am able to get the words out.

I assume my interns will join me in my dance, but instead they all stare at me with dead eyes. I have not seen such miserable faces since the Great Siege of Slupsk, when the children were told they must butcher and eat their pet rats.

"I can't believe you took the money," Claire whispers. "How could you just sell out like that?"

There are tears in her eyes; slowly, it dawns on me why she is so upset.

"I forgot to haggle," I admit. "It was stupid. I should have demanded even more of their sweet, sweet dollars."

Claire bangs her tiny fist against the wall.

"How could you be so *selfish?*" she says. "It's disgusting! I mean . . . what would Sarah say?"

I squint at her, confused. Sarah would be proud, of course. She would not join my dance, because her leg was lame and it shamed her. But she would clap her hands in time while I did my rich-man jig.

"I do not understand why you are upset," I admit to Claire. "Is it because you want some portion of my moneys?"

She glares at me, her nostrils flared like angry horse.

"We didn't join your company for money," she seethes. "We joined because we believed in you!"

I look over at the interns.

"So none of you want money?"

They look at the ground, their faces slightly red.

"I wouldn't mind some money," one of them mumbles.

"Is fair," I say, after some thought. "I will give you each bonus of ten dollars."

The interns cheer.

"Also," I announce, "from this day forth, you all shall have your freedom. Go! You are emancipate!"

"You're the worst," Claire says to me.

She starts to pack up all of her belongings: her folding

computer, her other computer, her tablet machine, her shiny talking phone. Something gradually occurs to me.

"Oh," I say. "I forgot. You are wealthy."

Claire turns around and stares at me. Her face is pale.

"Excuse me?"

"That is why you do not care for money. Because you already have so much of it. For you, all of life is happy game."

Her eyes begin to twitch.

"That is so *rude*," she says. "Life's about more than *money*, Herschel!"

"Yes," I say. "For those who already have it."

She shakes her head with disgust.

"You know what?" she tells me. "You're just like Simon."

It is six weeks later when I see my great-great-grandson. I have moved into wide brownstone on his block, so I knew such a meeting was inevitable. But the encounter is still surprising, because it is four in the morning.

At first we pretend not to see each other. But there are no other people outside at this hour, and so it is hard to keep up ruse.

"Hello," I say eventually.

"Hey," he says. "Nice chain."

I smile proudly. I had always dreamed of owning jewelry, so after buying house and crate of herring, I treated myself to necklace. It is simple, modest piece, just fifty golden links and my name spelled out in gems, with the *S* switched to dollar sign, so that it reads "Her$chel."

"I got it inside black-man store," I tell him. "They are the only ones who understood my style."

"It's cool you're doing so well," Simon says. "Congrats."

I nod. I am waiting for him to ask me what my chain costs, but for some reason he does not do this.

"My chain cost seven thousand dollars," I inform him.

"Congrats," he says again.

There is something I want to ask him, but I do not know how to say it.

"Simon," I say, "is there something wrong with the air on this street?"

He looks confused.

"The air?"

"Ever since I move here, I have been having problems with my breathing. It happens when I am trying at night to sleep. My heart becomes fast and I cannot fill up my lungs. I think there is possibly poison in the air."

Simon nods.

"They're called panic attacks," he says. "I get them all the time. They probably run in the family."

He takes out silver flask.

"Try some of this," he says.

"Do I look like Irishman?"

"Just think of it as medicine."

I close my eyes, hold my nose, and drink from the bottle. The taste is horrible, but after several swallows, I must admit, my breathing becomes easier.

"I do not understand what is happening to me," I confess to

Simon. "Tonight I ate eleven cans of herring, one after the other. Then I took hot bath with soap, like fancy king. But I could not enjoy it. My heart kept racing. Whenever I closed my eyes, I saw the dying men of Slupsk. I imagined them pointing at me with angry faces, cursing me for having so much pleasure."

"Sounds like you're getting a guilt complex."

"What is guilt complex?"

"It's something that happens to rich people."

"What is the cure?"

Simon shrugs. "You could donate some money to charity."

"Yes, okay, but that is not going to happen, so tell me other options."

Simon thinks. "Well, you could try to make a difference somehow."

I think of Claire and the people in the Vortex Factory and how they are trying to change the world. "I have no MFA," I say, "or PhD."

"You could go get one," he suggests. "I mean, they're expensive, but I'm sure you could afford it."

"I would rather have more jewels," I admit.

I sit down on stoop and massage my temples.

"Perhaps I will become freegan?" I suggest. "Can freegans eat herring?"

"I don't think so."

"Never mind." It is very cold, and so I decide to take more sips from flask. "Perhaps we pray."

Simon raises his eyebrows.

"What?"

"We must pray," I tell him. "That is why we feel guilt. We have received so many blessings, far more than we deserve, and it is wrong that we have not said thanks to God."

"Herschel, I already told you. I don't believe in that stuff. Besides..."

He averts his eyes.

"What is it?" I say.

He looks down at his feet.

"Well, I've never done it before. I'm not even sure I know how."

I lay my palm upon his shoulder.

"There is no wrong way to pray to Hashem," I tell him. "Just speak what is in your heart."

Simon remains still for long time. Then he nods slowly, closes his eyes, and kneels.

"Why are you kneeling?" I shout. "Are you Christian now? Stand up before God sees you!"

He jumps to his feet.

"I thought you said there was no wrong way to pray?"

"Yes, well, okay, but you cannot kneel! That is like slapping God's face. It is horrible what you have done."

I spit on the ground.

"Sorry," he says.

"Is fine, is fine," I say.

I catch my breath and lay my palm again upon his shoulder.

"Just close your eyes," I tell him. "And speak your heart. Remember, there is no wrong way to pray."

Simon nods, closes his eyes, and begins to speak.

"Dear God—"

"Are you insane?" I shout. "You would slap God's face with English words?"

Simon throws up his hands in frustration.

"You said there were no wrong words!"

"Is terrible thing that you have done."

"Okay, okay," he says. "I'm sorry. Let me try again."

I lay my palms once more upon his shoulders.

"There is no wrong way," I remind him.

He nods, hesitates, and then tries for the third time.

"Okay. Um... *Baruch atah Adonai Eloheinu melekh ha'olam... ha'motzi lehem...min ha-aretz?*" He smiles at me. "Was that all right?"

"That was prayer for bread," I say. "It makes no sense why you would say it. Where is the bread? I see no bread here. That was madness, your prayer for bread."

"How about this?" Simon suggests. "I'll tell you what I want to say to God and you can translate it for him."

I think about this plan.

"Is fine," I say.

He sits down beside me.

"Where do I start?" he mumbles. "Okay. Um...tell him, I'm sorry I played 2 Live Crew at my bar mitzvah party. And that I haven't been to synagogue in years...and that I pretended to be Christian once in college to get free barbecue..."

"Slow down," I say. "I am only up to '2 Live Crew.'"

"I'll just sum it up," Simon says. "Tell him...I'm sorry for taking everything for granted."

I close my eyes and whisper it in Jewish language.

"I have told Hashem," I say. "Is fine."

The sun is coming up, but I am still shivering. The gold chain feels like ice against my flesh. When my teeth start to chatter, Simon takes off purple scarf and hands it to me.

"What are you doing?"

"It's freezing out."

"I am not one who takes charity," I remind him.

"Just take it."

I am putting on scarf when I catch sight of Statue of Liberty. She is staring right at me through parted clouds.

"Is fine?" I whisper to her.

She smiles at me, her right fist raised in triumph.

"Is fine," I hear her say.

GUY WALKS INTO A BAR

So a guy walks into a bar one day and he can't believe his eyes. There, in the corner, there's this one-foot-tall man, in a tiny tuxedo, playing a sonata on a little piano.

So the guy asks the bartender, "Where'd he come from?"

And the bartender's, like, "There's a genie in the men's room who grants wishes."

So the guy runs into the men's room and, sure enough, there's this genie. And the genie's, like, "Your wish is my command." So the guy's, like, "Okay, I wish for world peace." And there's this big cloud of smoke — and then the room fills up with geese.

So the guy walks out of the men's room and he's, like, "Hey, bartender, I think your genie might be hard of hearing."

And the bartender's, like, "No kidding. You think I wished for a twelve-inch pianist?"

So the guy processes this. And he's, like, "Does that mean you wished for a twelve-inch *penis?*"

And the bartender's, like, "Yeah. Why, what did you wish for?"

And the guy's, like, "World peace."

So the bartender is understandably ashamed.

And the guy orders a beer like everything is normal, but it's obvious that something has changed between him and the bartender.

And the bartender's, like, "I feel like I should explain myself further."

And the guy's, like, "You don't have to."

But the bartender continues, in a hushed tone. And he's, like, "I have what's known as penile dysmorphic disorder. Basically, what that means is I fixate on my size. It's not that I'm small down there. I'm actually within the normal range. Whenever I see it, though, I feel inadequate."

And the guy feels sorry for him. So he's, like, "Where do you think that comes from?"

And the bartender's, like, "I don't know. My dad and I had a tense relationship. He used to cheat on my mom, and I knew it was going on, but I didn't tell her. I think it's wrapped up in that somehow."

And the guy's, like, "Have you ever seen anyone about this?"

And the bartender's, like, "Oh yeah, I started seeing a therapist four years ago. But she says we've barely scratched the surface."

So, at around this point, the twelve-inch pianist finishes up his sonata. He walks over to the bar and climbs onto one of the stools. And he's, like, "Listen, I couldn't help but overhear the end of your conversation. I never told anyone this before, but my dad and I didn't speak the last ten years of his life."

And the bartender's, like, "Tell me more about that." And he pours the pianist a tiny glass of whiskey.

And the twelve-inch pianist is, like, "He was a total monster. Beat us all. Told me once I was an accident."

And the bartender's, like, "That's horrible."

And the twelve-inch pianist shrugs. And he's, like, "You know what? I'm over it. He always said I wouldn't amount to anything, because of my height? Well, now look at me. I'm a professional musician!"

And the pianist starts to laugh, but it's a forced kind of laughter, and you can see the pain behind it. And then he's, like, "When he was in the hospital, he had one of the nurses call me. I was going to go see him. Bought a plane ticket and everything. But before I could make it back to Tampa..."

And then he starts to cry. And he's, like, "I just wish I'd had a chance to say goodbye to my old man."

And all of a sudden there's this big cloud of smoke — and a beat-up Plymouth Voyager appears!

And the pianist is, like, "I said 'old man,' not 'old van'!"

And everybody laughs. And the pianist is, like, "Your genie's hard of hearing."

And the bartender says, "No kidding. You think I wished for a twelve-inch pianist?"

And as soon as the words leave his lips, he regrets them. Because the pianist is, like, "Oh my God. You didn't really want me."

And the bartender's, like, "No, it's not like that." You know, trying to backpedal.

And the pianist smiles ruefully and says, "Once an accident, always an accident." And he drinks all of his whiskey.

And the bartender's, like, "Kevin, I'm sorry. I didn't mean that."

And the pianist smashes his whiskey glass against the wall and says, "Well, I didn't mean *that*."

And the bartender's, like, "Whoa, calm down."

And the pianist is, like, "Fuck you!" And he's really drunk, because he's only one foot tall and so his tolerance for alcohol is extremely low. And he's, like, "Fuck you, asshole! Fuck you!"

And he starts throwing punches, but he's too small to do any real damage, and eventually he just collapses in the bartender's arms.

And suddenly he has this revelation. And he's, like, "My God, I'm just like him. I'm just like him." And he starts weeping.

And the bartender's, like, "No, you're not. You're better than he was."

And the pianist is, like, "That's not true. I'm worthless!"

And the bartender grabs the pianist by the shoulders and says, "Dammit, Kevin, listen to me! My life was hell before you entered it. Now I look forward to every day. You're so talented and kind and you light up this whole bar. Hell, you light up my whole life. If I had a second wish, you know what it would be? It would be for you to realize how beautiful you are."

And the bartender kisses the pianist on the lips.

So the guy, who's been watching all this, is surprised, because he didn't know the bartender was gay. It doesn't bother him; it just catches him off guard, you know? So he goes to the bathroom, to give them a little privacy. And there's the genie.

So the guy's, like, "Hey, genie, you need to get your ears fixed."

And the genie's, like, "Who says they're broken?" And he opens the door, revealing the happy couple, who are kissing and gaining strength from each other.

And the guy's, like, "Well done."

And then the genie says, "That bartender's tiny penis is going to seem huge from the perspective of his one-foot-tall boyfriend."

And the graphic nature of the comment kind of kills the moment.

And the genie's, like, "I'm sorry. I should've left that part unsaid. I always do that. I take things too far."

And the guy's, like, "Don't worry about it. Let's just grab a beer. It's on me."

FAMILY BUSINESS

I love my father, but sometimes he can get on my nerves. It's hard to explain why exactly. It's just little things he does, here and there, that bother me. For example, sometimes he shits into his hands and then throws the shit into my face while jumping up and down and screaming. I know he's just trying to be funny—and it *is* funny, I can see that. But there's just something about it that annoys me. I've asked him politely not to do it anymore, but I always get the same reaction. He just rolls his yellow eyes and says, "I'm sorry, your majesty."

My father's been calling me "your majesty" for as long as I can remember. He does it whenever I rinse off fruit before eating it, or catch grubs with a stick instead of with my fingers. Basically, he does it whenever I do anything differently than he does.

When I told him I was thinking about going to school, he didn't even respond. He just kept picking dirt out of his belly button like I wasn't even in the same tree as him.

"There's a human scientist on the bottom of the mountain," I explained. "He's interviewing chimpanzees to see if any have the aptitude to learn sign language."

"And you think they're going to pick *you?*" His silver back quaked with laughter. "I'd like to see *that.*"

"Why can't you just stay here?" my mother asked. "There are plenty of job opportunities. I talked to your uncle Mike and he said he'd help you find work at the shit pile."

"I don't know if I want to work at the shit pile," I said.

"Why the hell not?" my father snapped. "*I* work at the shit pile. Your cousins work at the shit pile. It's good, honest work."

"I know."

"Decent pay, great benefits."

"Dad, I know."

"You think you're too *good* for it?"

"No! Dad, relax. I'm just interested in sign language. I think it would be a cool thing to study."

"'A cool thing to study,'" he said mockingly. "Just tell me this: how much is it going to cost me?"

"Nothing. If I get accepted, it's a full ride. The humans pay for everything."

He snorted.

"Okay, so you get into this fancy program and spend years learning sign language. What are you supposed to do with that afterward? Teach?"

I looked to my mother for support, but she was already crouched behind my father, carefully grooming his buttocks. She's always been submissive to him. Sometimes I think that's why they got together in the first place.

"You know," my mother said, "if you're interested in humans, your father could put you in touch with Curly."

I sighed. Curly was one of my dad's hunting buddies, a half-blind chimp who lived beyond the swamp. Some reporters from *National Geographic* had followed him around for an article in the 1990s. In our little jungle, that qualified him as an expert on humans.

"I'd be happy to put you in touch with Curly," my father said. "He'll be able to introduce you to the right people."

"That's okay," I said.

My mother glared at me.

"Why won't you let your father help you?"

I took a deep breath.

"Okay, fine," I said. "I'll talk to Curly."

"You know," my mother said, "your father was pretty big in the human world when he was young."

She nudged his giant belly.

"Tell him about the time you met you-know-who."

"Oh, I don't know," my father said, waving his paws around in a pantomime of reluctance.

"Please!"

"Oh, all right. So, this one time, I'm hanging out in my nest, when Jane pops over—"

"He means Jane Goodall," my mother whispered.

My father grinned, thrilled that his name-drop had landed.

"So Jane opens her banana crate," he continued. "And she says to me, 'How about a banana?' And so *I* say, 'How about *many* bananas?'"

My mother laughed hysterically. My father's been telling us his Goodall anecdote for years, and she always acts like it's her first time hearing it.

"What does that even mean?" I asked. "'Many bananas'? That's not even a joke."

My parents ignored me.

"I'll put you in touch with Curly," my father said again. "He'll introduce you to the right people."

My mother smiled at me.

"It's a good thing your dad's so well connected, huh?"

I turned to my father. "Where did you say you met Jane Goodall?"

His chewing slowed to a stop.

"My nest," he said.

"So, on top of a tree?"

"Yeah," my father said, avoiding eye contact. "On top of a tree."

"That's pretty interesting. Because the trees we nest in are very tall. And humans usually aren't that great at climbing."

My mother shot me a warning look, but I kept going.

"She must have been pretty *athletic* to make it all the way up to your nest. And to carry a crate with her, no less, one that was filled with, as you say, 'many bananas'—that's *really* impressive."

"I don't know what to tell you," my father said tensely. "That's how it happened."

I could hear my mother's nostrils flaring, but I pressed on.

"I always knew your friend Jane was smart, but I had no idea she was also the strongest human in the history of—"

A dark brown clump flew into my face. I coughed and choked, doubled over from the stench. When I looked up, I saw my mother standing over me, her little paw caked with shit.

"Don't you *ever* disrespect your father like that again," she whispered.

"I'm sorry," I mumbled. "Where'd he go?"

"He's in his tree," she said, pointing at a nearby baobab. "I think you should climb up and talk to him."

I looked up at his nest. My dad was barking at the moon, beating his flabby chest in a show of strength. It was embarrassing to watch.

"If he wants to talk," I said, "then he can climb down."

My mother stared at me angrily for a moment—then galloped off screaming into the night.

"I met with the scientists," I told my parents the next day. "They said I was the smartest chimp they'd ever seen."

"La-di-da," my father said. My mother was standing behind him, in her usual grooming position. Neither looked up at me.

"They tested me on memory, pattern recognition, and object permanence," I told them. "There were dozens of chimps, but I scored the highest."

"Good for you," my father grumbled, his voice thick with sarcasm.

Nobody said anything for a while. Eventually, my mother broke the silence.

"It was a big day at the shit pile," she said. "Your father found three grubs."

He grunted with pleasure, clearly relieved to be the center of attention again.

"The trick is to feel around in the shit," he told her proudly. "The grubs are sometimes at the bottom, so you need to reach down to the bottom."

"You're so smart," my mother said. "The smartest, most wonderful—"

"I'm flying to Stanford tomorrow," I interrupted.

My mother swallowed. For the first time all day, she looked up from my father's butt.

"How many jungles away is that?" she asked.

"I'm not sure," I told her. "It's in a human country called the U.S.A."

"A *human country?*" she repeated, her eyes wide with fear. "Like Zimbabwe?"

"Yeah," I said. "But bigger."

"Bigger than Zimbabwe?" my father snorted. "Not likely."

"Dad, it's, like, ten times bigger than Zimbabwe."

"Then how come I've never heard of it?"

"Anyway," I said, "the helicopter leaves at sunrise. I just snuck out of my cage for a minute to say goodbye."

My mom was trying hard to stay calm, but I could tell she was upset by the way her ears kept twitching.

"Mom, come on," I said. "Don't whimper. This is my chance to get out of this town. To see the world."

My father stood up suddenly and roared.

"Then *go!*" he shouted, his thick fur bristling. "Go have fun with your fancy human friends!" He smiled widely, baring his canines. "Just don't come crawling back to me when you fail."

II)

I always enjoy visiting the White House.

My colleague, Professor Fitzbaum, and I get dragged to so many tedious events. Fund-raisers, lectures, book signings—it can get pretty tiresome. The White House, though, is different.

It's dignified, refined. The truth is, it's one of the very few places I feel at home.

I was practicing my speech on the lawn when the First Lady stopped by to chat.

"Hello," she signed to me.

"Hello," I signed back.

I always enjoy our conversations. She patted me on the head and then took the stage to introduce me.

"Ladies and gentlemen, in honor of Earth Day, we have a very special speaker. Please 'go ape' for... Professor Chimpsky!"

It was time for my address. I nodded solemnly at Professor Fitzbaum, and the two of us took the stage.

"Thank you," I signed to the First Lady, raising my left paw to my lips. "Thank you. Thank you. Thank you."

I scanned the White House lawn. There were dozens of cameras trained on me, broadcasting my speech to humans all over the world. I cracked my knuckles, determined to do my species proud.

"Environment good," I began. "Peace. Earth Day. Hello. Peace. Me chimpanzee."

I waited for Fitzbaum to translate, then continued.

"Peace friends. We friends. Chimpanzee and people. Me chimpanzee. Environment good. Chimpanzee. Peace. Thank you. Goodbye. Chimpanzee."

Professor Fitzbaum finished translating, and the crowd burst into applause. The speech had been an enormous success— far greater than I had even hoped. It was the pinnacle of my entire career. Still, as usual, I had trouble enjoying my triumph. In moments like these, my thoughts always turned to my parents. I hadn't had any contact with them since the day I left the jungle. I didn't miss them, exactly. But part of me wished they could see how far I'd come. In just five years, I'd amassed more accolades than any chimp in history. My mastery of sign language was so vast and fluent, it had earned Professor Fitzbaum a MacArthur Genius Grant. My face had appeared in every magazine on earth, from the *Journal of Primatology* to *Parade*. My father, of course, didn't live near any newsstands. He'd never know how far his son had come.

A caterer set down a tray of champagne flutes. Fitzbaum usually limits my alcohol intake, but he was busy talking to reporters. I grabbed two flutes and tossed them back.

Across the lawn, the First Lady was talking to her daughters. When the younger one asked her a question, she answered patiently, smiling and nodding. I could tell she was a wonderful parent, the kind that always validated her children and never threw her shit into their faces.

There wasn't any more champagne poured out, so I grabbed a bottle from a nearby table. I was starting to feel a bit light-headed, but I didn't care. Earth Day came only once a year, after all.

"Hello," I signed to some nearby humans. "Hello. Hello."

They didn't understand me. What did it matter? I was almost finished with my champagne when Professor Fitzbaum finally returned. His eyes were wide and his movements frantic.

"Stop," he signed to me. "No."

I sighed. Fitzbaum and I have an excellent relationship. But sometimes he can be unreasonable.

"Earth Day," I explained. "Hello. Earth Day."

"No understand," he replied.

I threw up my hands in exasperation. It's not my fault he only taught me fifty signs.

"Give," he said, pointing at the bottle. *"Give."*

I looked around and saw that a crowd had formed. There were dignitaries, reporters, and—most troubling of all—a man holding a dart gun. I stamped my feet in frustration. Everyone was overreacting.

I was trying to sign something to that effect when I lost hold of my champagne bottle. It shattered on the ground. I jumped onto a table to avoid the flying glass shards and collided with a large ice sculpture of a globe. I don't remember much after that. Just the sound of shouting, the smell of grass, and a sharp little pain in my thigh.

I woke up in a cage.

At first I thought that I was alone. But as my vision adjusted, I became aware of a shadowy figure in the corner. It was another chimpanzee—old, obese, and out of breath. The hair on his back was thinning and the skin underneath was covered in dark red splotches. His face was dotted with insects, but he made no attempt to swat the bugs away. He just sat there in silence as they crawled up his nose and into his sunken eyes.

I walked across the cage and cautiously thrust out my paw.

"Hello," I said. "Nice to meet you."

"Me Charley," he said through labored breaths. "Charley the Chimp."

I assumed that he was joking. Charley the Chimp was

famous—an international movie star. His "Chimp Champion" videos had grossed millions in the 1980s. Fitzbaum had shown me all his hits during a study on primate self-recognition.

"You can't be Charley the Chimp," I said. "That's impossible."

The old ape shrugged.

"Fine," he said. "Me prove it."

He reached for an apple, paused to catch his breath, and then tossed it through the bars of our cage. I watched in shock as it sailed across the facility and landed neatly in a distant wastebasket.

"Oh my God!" I said. "You're really him!"

He nodded tiredly.

"Charley...me...Charley."

He was clearly on something. Tranquilizers, probably. I sat down beside him and groomed his splotchy back.

"I've seen all of your movies," I told him. "*Slam Dunk Charley, Touchdown Charley, Strikeout Charley.* I even saw the lacrosse one."

He winced. "*Bounce Shot Charley.*"

"Yeah!"

"*Bounce Shot Charley* not so good," he admitted. "We run out of sports...movie not same level as others."

"I don't know," I said. "I thought it had its moments."

He smiled proudly.

"Sprinkler gag was okay," he conceded. "So, what you in for?"

I laughed.

"Oh, just a little episode at the White House. But I'm not here permanently."

He shook his head. "Everyone here permanently."

"Not me," I said. "My trainer's probably en route as we speak. We've been a duo for five years. We're like family."

Charley leaned in close. I could feel his hot breath on my face.

"Trainer not like family," he said. "Only family like family."

He looked off into the distance.

"I used to have trainer," he said. "We like brothers. He take me People's Choice. He take me Golden Globes. We wear matching suits—mine just like his, but smaller. Then one day, on set of *Karate Chop Charley*, I get confused and make one mistake during filming. Me here ever since."

"That's so unfair," I said. "What happened? Did you forget your part or something?"

"I rip testicles off actor. Throw across road."

"Oh."

Charley sighed.

"I not even get to finish movie. If you watch video close, they use backup chimp in tournament scene." He shook his head bitterly. "He never got kick right. Movie suffer for it."

I nodded sympathetically. This poor chimp had devoted his life to entertaining humans, and they'd thrown him away just like a broken toy. Could that really happen to me? I was starting to despair when Professor Fitzbaum walked into the room.

"Hello!" I signed. "Hello!"

I didn't want to make Charley jealous, but I couldn't resist a few celebratory hoots. My friend had come to get me, just like I knew he would.

"Thank you," I signed, raising my left paw to my lips. "Thank you. Hello. Love."

Professor Fitzbaum's hands remained rigidly by his sides. I wondered if he could see me in the shadows.

"Love!" I signed again. "Hello. Me chimpanzee. Good."

Fitzbaum took a step closer, and I winced. He wasn't alone. Behind him was the man with the dart gun.

"No," I signed passionately. "Stop. Please. Friends."

"I'm sorry," Fitzbaum said. "But my facilities can't accommodate a full-grown chimpanzee."

Charley laid his meaty palm on my shoulder. I felt a scalding tear roll down my face.

"Don't worry," Fitzbaum said. "You don't have to stay here." He grinned at me.

"I'm taking you home!"

I let out a scream as the man with the dart took aim.

III)

"Guess it didn't work out, huh?" my father said after our obligatory hug. "Well, don't say I didn't warn you." He looked the same, only slightly heavier and with a few more gray streaks on his back.

"It's okay," my mother told me. "I've already talked to Uncle Mike, and there's a position for you at the shit pile."

"Thanks, Mom."

She passed me a handful of grubs, and I felt my stomach turning. I didn't remember them being so unappetizing.

"What's the matter?" my father said, his mouth already full of hairy bugs. "Not fancy enough for you?"

"Jeez, Dad. I just got back. Please..."

My parents gasped and it took me a moment to figure out why. I'd been signing unconsciously as I spoke.

"What the hell are you doing?" my father asked.

"It's sign language," I explained. "It's actually not so hard. Look, I'll show you."

I tried to teach them "thank you," the easiest sign I knew, just a touch of the left paw to the lips.

"You follow any of that?" my father asked my mother.

"No," she said.

My father laughed.

"I can't believe you spent five years on that nonsense," he said. "What a waste."

"It wasn't a waste," I said defiantly. "I got to do all sorts of amazing things—things you wouldn't believe."

He folded his flabby arms across his chest.

"Like what?"

"I got to go to the White House."

"What's that?"

"It's where the president of the United States lives."

"You met the president?" my mother asked.

"Well...no," I admitted. "But I met his First Lady."

My father snorted.

"That's not the same thing."

"You know," my mother said, "your *father* once met a celebrity. Honey, tell him about the time you talked to you-know-who."

"Oh, I don't know," he said, waving his paws around.

"Please!"

"Oh, all right. So one time, I'm in my tree, and Jane—"

"He means Jane Goodall—"

A whirring noise sounded in the clearing below. I looked down and sighed. Fitzbaum was already searching for my replacement. His truck was loaded with various testing apparatuses. I recognized a large plastic box from the day we'd met. It was a simple pattern-recognition test. You climbed inside and watched as three colored orbs lit up. If you hit the corresponding levers in the correct order, you won a banana. I could still remember how Fitzbaum had beamed when I solved it on my very first try.

I heard some rustling in the trees around us. Dozens of chimps were balanced on high branches, watching Fitzbaum skeptically.

"Here, chimpy, chimpy," my old friend said, dragging the plastic box out of his truck. "Who wants to win a treat?"

My father snorted again.

"How hard could it be?"

"Extremely hard," I told him. "That test requires memory, dexterity, and problem-solving skills."

My father flicked his paw dismissively.

"Any monkey can push around some levers."

"Oh yeah?" I said. "Then why don't you try it?"

My mother climbed between us, but I kept on going, pointing aggressively at his face.

"If the test is so easy, why don't you climb inside the box and show me how it's done?"

My father looked around. The entire tribe was watching at this point.

"Fine," he said, grinning widely so the other chimps could see. "No sweat."

My mother squirmed as he leaped out of the branches and landed with a thud beside the box. Uncle Mike cheered and the other chimps joined in. My father wasn't the leader of our tribe, but he was a respected elder. I wondered if he knew what he was risking.

"I'll be back in a second," he called out confidently. "With *many* bananas!"

The tribe clapped and hooted as he climbed into the clear plastic cube.

From the moment the lights started flashing, it was obvious my father was outmatched. He tried to put on a brave face as he randomly poked the levers. But, within a couple of minutes, his frustration grew obvious. He let out a roar, grabbed a random lever, and pulled it as hard as he could. I smiled to myself as he yanked uselessly on it, his broad shoulders shaking with frustration. Eventually, he had no choice but to give up.

"Thing's broken," he muttered, avoiding eye contact with the crowd. I couldn't help but gloat as he started to climb out of the box.

"Not so easy, huh?" I said. He didn't respond. It was around this time I realized he was stuck.

"What's happening?" he asked, his consternation giving way to terror. "What's *happening?*"

I climbed down to a lower branch to get a better view. My father's stomach was wedged between two levers. His breaths were fast and shallow. Fitzbaum watched impassively from his truck, jotting down notes in his field binder.

A crack of thunder sounded, and the tribe quickly dispersed. My father watched with fear as his friends and brothers fled.

"How could you do this to him?" my mother shouted at me over the sound of pouring rain.

"I didn't do anything!" I shouted back. "He's the one who wanted to try the box!"

"He's old!" she screamed. "Can't you see that? He's *old*."

Professor Fitzbaum cursed at the rain, hopped into his truck, and drove out of sight. My father sat shivering in the cramped plastic cube. The water was up to his ankles and rising.

"Do something!" my mother yelled at me.

I hopped off the tree and galloped across the clearing.

"Dad!" I shouted. "If you suck in your stomach, I can pull you out!"

"Go away!" he screamed. "I don't need your help! Get out of here!"

The rain intensified, and my father started whimpering. The water was past his knees. I looked at my mother. She was jumping up and down in a panic.

I reached for my dad's paw, but he swatted me away. His eyes were wild, his movements frenzied. He was totally disoriented. The water was almost at his waist by the time I figured out a plan.

"Dad!" I shouted over the sound of falling branches. "I'm hungry."

He didn't respond, but he finally stopped thrashing.

"I'm hungry," I repeated. "I never ate dinner." I took a cautious step toward him. "I wish there were grubs I could eat."

My father's breathing slowed.

"There are grubs everywhere," he said.

I poked at the muddy ground, feigning confusion.

"I'm not good at it," I said over the sound of howling wind. "I need help from an expert—someone who knows about grubs and about shit."

My father's expression brightened.

"I can help," he said.

"Really? You wouldn't mind?"

"Nah," he said, his posture straightening slightly. "It's no big deal."

"Great! Suck in your stomach, and I'll pull you out."

"What?"

"So you can help me."

"Oh."

He sucked in his gut and I heaved on his arm, dragging him out of the box. He immediately thrust his paw into the ground.

"The trick is to reach down to the bottom. See?"

He pulled out a grub and handed it to me.

"Thanks," I said. I forced a smile and shoved the wriggling creature into my mouth. "Mmm. Delicious."

"Want another?" he said.

"Um...sure."

He reached back into the mud and pulled out a whole handful. I swallowed them as quickly as I could.

"You're good at hunting grubs," I told him. "I'm really impressed."

"I guess I'm okay at it," he murmured.

He beat his chest a couple of times. At some point, it had stopped raining.

"Come on," he said. "I'll groom you."

"You don't have to groom me."

He ignored my protests and squatted down behind me. I looked up and saw my mother looking down at me from a tree. She scrunched up her face as if trying to remember something. Then she thrust out her left paw and raised it briefly to her lips.

THE TRIBAL RITE OF THE
STROMBERGS

"Hmm."

"What?"

"Not sure about *qat*."

Jeremy looked up from the board with shock. His father had never questioned any of his words before. The old man's lead was usually so big that he let Jeremy put down anything he wanted—proper nouns, abbreviations, even the occasional swear word.

"It's a type of plant," Jeremy said. "I learned it on Words with Friends."

"What's that?"

"It's an app."

"Hmm," his father said.

Jeremy folded his arms and smirked. "You're welcome to challenge it."

His father picked at a loose wooden button on his cardigan.

"That's all right," he said, flicking his wrist. "I'll let you have it."

Jeremy grinned. His dad only had five tiles left and they were obviously doozies. He couldn't remember a game ever being this close. He'd come within ten points once, during college. But his father had just had his gallbladder removed and was woozy from a host of strong narcotics.

"Are we allowing foreign words?" his father asked.

Jeremy raised his eyebrows. Foreign words were never allowed. His dad was the one who'd taught him that rule.

"Of course not," he said.

"Hmm," his father said. "Then I guess . . . I'll pass."

They both glanced at the score pad. "Dad" was still ahead, 252–239. But "Jerm" was about to end the game.

" 'Ta,' " he said proudly.

"What?"

" 'Ta,' " Jeremy said. "T-A. Like *goodbye*."

He slid his final tile into place, a *T* before the *A* in *qat*. He'd set it up and things had played out perfectly.

"Challenge," his father said.

Jeremy laughed. "Seriously?"

"Challenge," his father repeated, his voice gruff with frustration.

Jeremy shook his head in disbelief. They'd both been using *ta* for years.

"Okay, fine."

He cracked open the Scrabble dictionary and showed his father *ta*.

"Here's *qat*, too," he said, flipping back a few pages.

His father scratched his scalp. He was still up eleven points, but they hadn't yet accounted for his remaining letters.

"Come on," Jeremy said. "Let me see 'em."

His father reluctantly turned over his rack. He had mostly vowels, predictably, three *A*s and an *E*. But one tile stood out, like a clump of gold in gravel: a jagged, ten-point Z.

"Yes!" Jeremy shouted, banging his fist against the table. "Holy shit, I can't believe it!"

He subtracted his dad's tiles from his score, added the amount to his own, and scribbled down the final tally.

Dad: 238, Jerm: 255!

He tore off the sheet and pocketed it. He couldn't wait to show it to his fiancée. She'd read his dad's textbook in college and considered him a genius. Her mind was about to be blown. He was posting a picture of the board to Instagram when he noticed that his father was undressing.

"Dad?" he said. "What are you doing?"

"I knew this day would come," he said. He stripped off his shirt and knelt on the ground, his naked arms stretched out in supplication.

"Club me to death," he begged. "And eat my body."

"Dad . . ."

"Eat my weakened body," his father said. "For I have become too old to live."

"Dad, come on," Jeremy said. "It's just one game. It doesn't have to be like this."

But he knew there were no alternatives. The Stromberg family had been practicing this rite for generations. He himself had witnessed his mother shove his grandmother onto an ice floe. They were on a ski trip in Vermont, and his grandmother had forgotten the name of the actor who played Frasier.

"It's not a big deal," his mother said through sobs. "Everybody forgets things sometimes."

The old woman shook her head stoically.

"Bathe me in sacred oils," she commanded. "And cast me out to burden you no more."

They'd fed Aunt Susan to a horse in Central Park when she

was only fifty. She'd promised to get her niece a summer internship at Bravo. But, when she called up the producer she used to date, he told her he was no longer with the network. Layoffs were looming and he'd taken a buyout. Susan was floored. She'd had ins at NBC for as long as she could remember. She'd dated assistants in her twenties, writers in her thirties, and executives in her forties. Now she didn't even know anyone who worked there.

"It's okay!" her niece insisted, as little tears formed in her eyes. "I don't even care about TV! I just wanted an excuse to live in New York this summer—"

"Feed me to beasts," Susan interrupted. "For I have outlived my purpose."

Grandma Edith had walked off a cliff on Thanksgiving after accidentally calling her granddaughter's black boyfriend Barack.

"It's no big deal," said the boyfriend, whose name was John. "I'm not offended."

But it was too late. Edith had already put on her New Balances and headed for the rocks.

Uncle Mort had taken the rite just two weeks ago. He was making some coffee for his daughter when a fuzzy voice blared from his dusty Dell computer, "You've got mail!"

"Oh my God," his daughter said. "You still have an AOL account?"

Mort's wrinkled face flushed with shame.

"You've got mail!" the voice repeated. "File's done."

Mort nodded once at his daughter, and she knew without asking what he wanted her to do. She led him quietly out of his house and drove him through Boca, to the ocean. He kissed her on the forehead and then marched into the surf, his chin held high, proud to be leaving the earth with dignity.

Jeremy didn't think that his father, though, was anywhere near that stage. He wasn't young, of course. But he was still pretty vibrant. Just last year he'd published his ninth book. Sure, it wasn't his most original work. (The *Journal of Anthropology* had called it a retread of *Tribes,* his one bestseller, now out of print.) Still, it was a real book, with footnotes and a cover and everything. So what if nobody wanted to buy it or read it?

"I know you're upset," Jeremy's father said. "But you have no choice. You must perform this holy rite." He rooted around in the living-room closet. "Where is that thing?" he muttered, rifling through a stack of old squash rackets. "Ah."

He handed his son an oblong slab of wood. The club had been in the Stromberg family for years. It was by far their most ancient possession, even older than the George Foreman Grill.

Jeremy held the club up to the light. The bulbous side was stained with horrible reddish streaks. He looked back at his father and saw that he was kneeling on the rug, his balding head bowed toward him.

"Congratulations on beating me in Scrabble."

Jeremy clenched his fists with anger.

"Why didn't you use your Z earlier? You played *aero* — that could have been *zero!*"

"What's done is done."

"I'm sorry," Jeremy said, his eyes already glossy. "I didn't know what I was doing."

"Yes, you did," his father said.

Jeremy let out a sob as he raised the club over his head.

DISTRACTIONS

"Who cares what Sparklegum12 thinks?" Kayla said. "He's just some random moron on the Internet."

"It's the very first comment," Gabe said. "As soon as people finish the story, they're going to see that comment and it's going to bias them."

He clenched his fists.

"It's going to *bias* them," he repeated.

"People love your story," Kayla said. "See? It's got four stars."

"Three and a half."

"Why can't you just be proud of yourself? It's the *Synecdoche Review*. You've been submitting there for years."

"I'm never submitting there again. First they make me change the ending, then they water down the opening paragraph, then they post a nasty comment at the very top of the comments, to make sure people hate the story because of the comments!"

He glanced at his MacBook and gasped. His half a star had vanished. He was down to a mere three.

"Fucking fuck!" he shouted.

Kayla sighed as Gabe paced around his studio, waving his arms at the ceiling.

"It's unbelievable! They always find a way to fuck me, every time."

"Who's 'they'?"

"The whole fucking literary establishment! They hate that I'm trying to do something new—it terrifies them! I'm sorry I didn't go to Iowa! I'm sorry my stories are actually original!"

He stopped pacing. At some point during his rant, Kayla had put on her coat.

"Where are you going?" he asked.

"Home," she said. "I thought we were going to cook lasagna and have sex. Instead, you threw a tantrum for three hours about a story in an online magazine that nobody even reads. I'm hungry, I'm tired, and I want to go to bed."

He reached for her arm, and she shook him away.

"I'm sorry that Sparklegum12 disliked your story," she said. "I'm sorry you can't finish your novel. I'm sorry you're not some famous celebrity writer. It doesn't mean the whole world's out to get you."

"You're right," Gabe said. "I've been acting crazy tonight."

"It's not just tonight."

"Who are you calling?"

"A cab."

"He's onto us," Kayla whispered as she ran out of Gabe's building, her iPhone pressed tightly to her ear.

"We know," said the voice on the other end.

"What do I do?"

"Just get here."

Kayla scanned the street. There was a phone booth on the corner of Myrtle and Bedford. She ran inside, dialed the secret code, and sank into the depths of Brooklyn.

She emerged minutes later in a torch-lit hall a hundred feet below the borough's surface. The council was already assembling. Kayla bowed with deference as they took their places on the dais. The bottom row was reserved for the editors of prestigious literary magazines. Above them sat representatives from all the major American publishing houses. On the top tier sat members of Congress, titans of industry, and the president of the United States. A giant flag hung behind them, featuring the association's logo: a picture of Gabe's face, bisected with a diagonal slash.

Kayla took a seat in the gallery, next to one of her fellow agents.

"Nice work with that comment," she said.

"Thanks," said Sparklegum12.

"Is he here yet?" Kayla asked.

"He's coming."

Thousands rose as the leader marched through a pair of large brass doors. His expression was unsettlingly grim.

"Where," he asked, "is Kayla?"

The blood drained from Kayla's face as she stood. The leader walked toward her, his silver cane clacking against the gleaming marble floor.

"You were given a simple task," he said. "To distract Gabe from our mission to destroy him."

"I'm trying my best," Kayla said.

The leader slapped her hard across the face. She fell to her knees and wept.

"You don't seem to realize what's at stake," he said. "Gabe's fiction could upend the entire literary establishment. His stories are so original—so unlike anything from Iowa—it could turn the world of letters on its head. And once he conquers that arena, his power will only grow. It starts with a few online stories. Then he finishes his novel. The next thing you know, he's become a figure so globally dominant, all mankind is crushed beneath his yoke. We must stop his rise!"

The conspirators murmured their assent. Since the moment Gabe first put pen to page, they'd done what they could to thwart his dreams.

They hired construction workers to drill outside his window every time he tried to write.

They created a phony law firm to hire him as a paralegal and fill up his weekdays with busywork.

They commissioned pornographers to create hard-core sex videos that catered to his specific tastes, and then sent him these videos, in the form of pop-up ads, whenever he was "on a roll," so that the urge to masturbate would force him to abandon his fiction.

They paid actors to pose as friends and invite him to parties every Saturday, so that he'd be too hungover to write on his one day off. And they sent him a series of girlfriends to distract him from his art with a mixture of affection and love.

Still, despite their efforts, Gabe hadn't abandoned his writing. He still threatened to collapse the status quo and tear apart the fabric of society.

The leader folded his arms across his chest.

"Where," he asked, "is the online fiction editor of the *Synecdoche Review*?"

A goateed man sheepishly raised his hand.

"Why did you publish his story?" the leader demanded.

The editor looked away. Tears were already streaming down his face.

"I'm sorry," he said. "It was just too good. If I'd rejected it, he would have known something was up. I thought that if I made the story worse by changing the ending, and watering down the first paragraph—"

The leader wrapped his fingers around the editor's neck.

"Please," gurgled the underling as he tried to pry the gloved hands from his throat. "Please."

The crowd watched in silence as the leader strangled the life out of his body. The editor kept struggling, but eventually his wriggling limbs went limp.

Kayla swallowed as some henchmen appeared and dragged away the corpse.

"Stop him," the leader told her. "Or else."

Kayla was lying awake in bed when she heard a soft knock on her door.

"Are you still up?" Gabe mumbled.

She let him into her apartment. He was holding a foil-wrapped platter.

"What's this?"

"I did the lasagna."

She looked up at her boyfriend; his eyes were as wide and fearful as a child's.

"I'm so sorry about before," he said. "I was being such an idiot."

He put down the lasagna and gave her a tentative hug. She put out some plates and forks and they began to eat in silence.

"It's still hot," Kayla said.

"I took a cab," he said. "I didn't want it to get cold."

She reached across the table and took his hand. He smiled with relief.

"What's that?" Kayla asked, pointing to a paperback in his coat pocket.

He took it out and showed it to her.

"Practice tests," he said. "For the LSATs."

"Seriously?"

Gabe blushed.

"I just signed up for it. I'm taking it on the twenty-fifth. I'm going to spend this month studying. Just...going all out every weekend."

She raised an eyebrow. "What about your novel?"

Gabe flicked his wrist.

"I think I'm done with that stuff for a while," he said. "It was distracting me from what's really important." He looked up at Kayla and saw that she was grinning.

"Why are you smiling?" he asked.

"No reason."

"Come on, tell me."

"I'm just happy," she said. "That's all."

PLAYED OUT

"Nice kicks," Dan said with a smirk.

I looked down and winced. I'd tried my best to wear cool clothes to Brooklyn, but Dan had zeroed in on my one lapse.

"The firm makes me wear loafers," I said. "Sucks, right?"

Dan ignored me. He'd taken out a bag of loose tobacco and was rolling himself a cigarette. I thought about asking to bum one but was terrified I might cough in front of him. There was only so much embarrassment I could take. I'd been with Dan for fifteen minutes, and my lameness had already earned me two eye rolls, one for mispronouncing "Nostrand Avenue" and the other for quoting *Modern Family*. Add my Ferragamos to the mix, and it was a miracle Dan was still willing to be seen with me.

"So why'd you move out of Astoria?" I asked.

Dan rolled his eyes harder than he had all night, his lashes fluttering almost audibly.

"It's so played out. It used to be chill. Now all anyone cares about is who's got the newest iPad. It's turning into another Park Slope. Just totally fucking bougie."

I smiled. Only Dan would consider Astoria bourgeois. But that was the kind of guy he'd always been. At Dalton, when I was cramming for my SATs, he was sneaking out to unannounced Strokes concerts. He dropped out of Skidmore after less than a month and moved straight to Williamsburg, a full decade before it became cool. Now he lived in a neighborhood that was so hip I'd never even heard of it. He was always miles ahead of everyone and light-years ahead of me.

"So, how's the band going?" I asked.

"We're working on an EP," he said. "But it's hard to rehearse, now that Dave's all Mr. Corporate."

I nodded. Dave worked for the teachers' union, but Dan's definition of *corporate* was wide enough to include anything with steady hours. He'd had only one job in his life—running the guest list at a rock venue in Bushwick. He'd quit when they banned smoking.

"Hey, do you remember that time in ninth grade?" I asked, eager to reminisce. "When Mr. Hurwitz caught us with those beers?"

"Fucking Hurwitz," Dan said, his rage untouched by the years.

I closed my eyes and luxuriated in the memory. Dan and I hiding behind a water tower, Pabsts in hand, trying not to laugh while our balding teacher shouted in the distance. It was the last time I'd felt cool enough to be his friend.

"I wonder what that fucker's up to now," Dan said.

I swallowed. "You didn't hear?"

"Hear what?"

"Jeez," I said. "Well, I'm sorry to be the one to tell you, but Mr. Hurwitz actually passed away."

Dan laughed. "How'd that happen?"

"I think it was just his time. At the memorial service they said he was eighty-seven."

Dan squinted at me.

"You went to his *memorial* service?"

"Yeah, me and Dave stopped by after work. It was nice. His daughters spoke. There's pictures on Facebook if you want to check it out."

Dan shrugged. "I'm not on Facebook."

He knelt over a manhole and yanked off the heavy metal lid.

"Come on," he said. "I'll show you my new place."

"I've never been in a sewer before," I admitted.

Dan snorted. "Why am I not surprised?"

I followed him down the ladder, the rusted rungs scraping against my palms.

"So what's it like living down here?" I asked.

"You mean, like, without a Whole Foods?"

I bit my lip. Sometimes, with Dan, it was safest not to speak at all.

He hopped off the ladder and landed with a sloshy thud. "You coming or what?"

I felt something bristly brush against my ankles. "Are there rats down here?"

"For now," Dan said. "Once this place gets gentrified, who knows?"

"And you're the only human?"

"Yes," he said in a sarcastic schoolboy monotone. "I am the only human."

"Cool!" I said. "Cool."

I said goodbye mentally to my Ferragamos and leaped into the darkness. The water was icy, with the troubling consistency of stew. The smell was unimaginable, so pungent I could taste it. It was completely dark except for a small reddish flame; at some point, Dan had lit another cigarette.

"So this is the practice space," Dan said as we waded through the muck. "And the bedroom's over there, between those pipes." He picked up a metal spike. "You hungry?"

I shook my head and watched as he jabbed the murky water with his weapon. Dan had never been an athlete and his thrusts were pretty clumsy. Eventually, though, after ten or fifteen minutes, I heard a squashing noise. He pulled his spike out of the water and smirked at his catch: a wriggling, screeching eel. The creature lunged for his face and he bashed its head against a pipe.

"Fucking eel," he said. "Relax."

He lifted the dangling creature to his mouth and bit a chunk out of its middle. Black blood spurted onto his skinny jeans.

"Want some?" he asked.

"That's okay."

"I could, like, put processed sugar on it or whatever, to make it taste like McDonald's."

"What?"

"Never mind," Dan said. He was about to take another bite when the eel regained consciousness and lunged at his face again.

"Aaaaah!" Dan screamed as it bit into his flesh. "*Aaaaaaaaaah!*"

He flailed his arms as the eel thrashed around, its jagged teeth pressed into his cheek.

"Kill it!" he screamed. "Kill it!"

I grabbed Dan's spike and tried to detach the eel from his face.

"Kill it!" Dan screamed. "Kill it! Kill it! Kill it! Kill it!"

"I'm trying!"

"Kill it!" Dan repeated. *"Aaaaaaah! Kill it!"*

I jabbed the spike into the monster's yellow eyes. It shrieked and slithered down into the sewage. A rat dragged the carcass out of sight.

"Hey!" Dan shouted as the rodent ran off with his meal. "Hey!"

I looked up at my friend. His expression was impassive, but I could tell he was in pain. His bruised hands were trembling and he was bleeding from a large gash in his face.

If I wanted to get him out of the sewer, I was going to have to strategize.

"Dan," I said cautiously, "I don't know about this place."

He cocked his chin. "What's wrong with it?"

I hesitated. "It's sort of... played out."

"Played out?"

"Yeah," I said. "It used to be chill? Now all anyone cares about is who's got the newest eel. It's turning into another Park Slope."

Dan nodded slowly. "I guess it has gotten sort of bougie."

"It's totally bougie!" I said, rolling my eyes for emphasis. "Now come on, let's go to that party."

"There's a party?"

"Yeah! It's in this old brick building called Mount Sinai. It's a pretty crazy scene. They've got all these beds set up. And people walking around in gowns. Lots of drugs."

"Sounds pretty chill."

He followed me up the ladder and I Ubered us to the ER.

"This is pretty cool," he said as some orderlies cut off his clothing and sedated him.

"It's cool," I assured him.

A nurse dressed his wounds and slid some paper slippers on his feet.

"Nice kicks," I said. Dan smiled proudly and drifted off to sleep.

RIP

Rip reached into his minifridge and pulled out a Four Loko. The government had banned the beverage months ago, claiming its high caffeine and alcohol content caused liver damage. But he'd saved one can to drink on a special occasion. And now, for the first time since graduating, he finally had something worth celebrating.

At 12:00 a.m. EST, he had officially achieved funding on Kickstarter for his jazz blog. Starting tomorrow, he'd be sticking it to the mainstream jazz media one post at a time.

His parents had offered to get him an internship at *Jazz Masters Monthly* (they were friends with the editor in chief). But Rip wasn't interested in working for a soulless place like that. How could a corporate-owned magazine possibly be an authority on *jazz*? He'd done some digging online and found out that the same company that owned *Jazz Masters Monthly* owned *Cat Fancy*. Who gave a shit about cats?

"Their office is in midtown," his mother told him over the phone. "So be sure to wear a suit."

"I don't own a suit," Rip told her proudly.

"Buy one," she begged. "Please, just put it on the card."

Rip said he would but never got around to it. Instead, the night before the interview, he stayed up late jamming with Fish and Stinky. They'd been in an experimental acid trio at Brown called the Ketchup Dilemma, and even though they'd been out of school for five years, they still made jamming a priority. They were taking a break between songs to snort some Adderall when the answer to Rip's problems suddenly popped into his head. He didn't need to put on some suit and take the G to the L to Manhattan every day. He could start his own magazine, on the World Wide Fucking Web. At 4:00 a.m. he sent an email to the editor, canceling the interview and wishing him luck with his "corporate rag." His friends laughed and cheered as he CC'd his parents and clicked Send. Forget being an intern for some monthly magazine. He was going to be the founder of a daily one.

Now, after sixty days of waiting, he'd finally raised the funds he needed to get started. He had six thousand dollars to pay the Web designer, one thousand to buy albums to review, and thirty-five hundred to make promotional T-shirts. He also had an ice-cold Four Loko in his hand. He reclined on his futon and poured the sour liquid down his throat. He was tired, but he didn't want to sleep. He couldn't wait for tomorrow.

Rip woke up with a horrible taste in his mouth. He opened the blinds and recoiled at the brightness of the sun. It was noon, if not later, and he was starving. He rummaged through the futon, found his phone, and called up Stinky.

"Breakfast?" he asked.

"It's two p.m.," Stinky said.

Rip laughed.

"So?"

"I'm at work."

Rip was confused.

"When did you get a job?"

"I gotta go," Stinky said. "That's a client on the other line."

"A client?" Rip stood up with excitement. "That mean you're dealing again?"

"What? No. I'm in advertising."

Rip felt his throat go dry.

"Stinky," he said, "what's going on?"

"It's Stanley," said Stinky. "And I'm sorry, but I have to go."

Rip staggered into the bathroom and gasped. He'd never been able to grow a beard before; the hairs always came in unevenly. Now his entire face was covered in thick black fur. It was terrifying but also pretty cool. He looked sort of like the drummer from the Jacob Fred Jazz Odyssey. He was about to post a picture on Instagram when he noticed something disconcerting. The front of his beard was black and lush, but the sides were thinning and flecked with streaks of gray.

"Fuck," Rip said.

His phone began to vibrate in his hands. He waited for it to stop, but it kept on throbbing, like a bird trying to escape from his clutches. Eventually, after five or six minutes, the shaking subsided and a line of text flashed nightmarishly onto the screen. Rip's eyes widened. He had over four thousand voice mails.

He brewed a pot of stale Blue Bottle and spent the afternoon catching up. Stinky was managing accounts at BBDO, one of the biggest international advertising agencies on earth. Fish had gone to law school, taken a job at White & Case, and moved into a brownstone in Park Slope. His sister was married with a daughter, and his parents had moved to Boca Raton. The Jacob

Fred Jazz Odyssey had changed lineups. The year was 2014. Rip wasn't twenty-seven anymore.

He was thirty.

"Sorry I'm late," Rip said. "The G took forever."

"Why didn't you take a cab?" Fish asked.

"What?"

"A *cab*," Stinky said. "So you'd be on time."

Rip stared blankly at his friends. He was confused and frightened.

"Well, we've lost our table," Fish said, throwing his manicured hands up in frustration. "So I guess Ruby Foo's it is."

"Whoa," Rip said. "That place is kind of pricey. Can't we just, like, go to Burritoville? They've got free chips and those sauces."

His friends ignored him and bounded south, their black loafers slapping against the pavement.

"I'm so hungover," Rip said. "That Four Loko fucked me up big-time."

Fish nodded. "You should do a cleanse."

"A what?"

"A cleanse," Fish said. "I've been on one for six weeks. No alcohol, no caffeine, no refined sugar. I feel fantastic."

They got to Ruby Foo's and sat down in a booth.

"Sparkling or tap?" asked a waiter.

"Sparkling," Fish and Stinky said in unison.

The waiter carefully poured them Pellegrino. His cheeks

were full and rosy, and some pimples were clustered around his hairline. Rip winced at the realization that the waiter was younger than he was.

"You guys know I slept for three years, right?" he asked his friends.

Stinky sipped his Pellegrino. "You should see a doctor," he said. "Someone good."

"My guy's fantastic," Fish said. "He made *New York*'s Hundred Best this year. What insurance do you have?"

"I'm not sure."

"You're not *sure?*"

Rip felt his cheeks flush beneath his beard. He opened the menu and anxiously scanned the prices.

"Do you think they'll let me have just the extra chicken, but not the salad?"

"What?" Fish said.

"It says, Chinese cabbage salad, fourteen dollars, but then there's six dollars if you want to add chicken. Do you think they'll let me just have the chicken? For six dollars?"

"You want a plate of loose chicken?"

"I mean... I don't know."

Stinky and Fish started talking about the new Malcolm Gladwell book.

"His thesis is pretty counterintuitive," Stanley said.

"That's why it works," Fish said.

"Guys, I slept for a long time," Rip said. "I'm scared."

The waiter returned to the table.

"Have you gentlemen decided?"

Rip cleared his throat.

"Can I just have the chicken that you can add to the cabbage salad but not the salad?"

"Excuse me?"

Rip stared down at his lap. He could feel his friends' eyes on him.

"Never mind," he mumbled. "I'm not hungry."

The waiter turned to Stinky.

"And for you, sir?"

"Sashimi," Stinky said.

Fish held up two fingers.

"Two sashimi," the waiter confirmed. "Good choice."

"I hate it when they comment," Fish said when the waiter was out of earshot.

Stinky nodded in agreement. "It's unprofessional."

Rip looked on dumbly as his friends resumed their conversation. Their words were strange to him: Roth IRA, Shelter Island, Roberto Cavalli. He couldn't follow any of it.

His stomach rumbled as his best friends ate their sashimi. He hadn't eaten breakfast, or any other meals, for several years, but he was too embarrassed to ask them for a bite. Within a few minutes, every sliver of fish was gone.

"So what are you guys doing tonight?" Rip asked during a lull in a discussion of gyms.

"What do you mean?" Fish asked.

"After this," Rip said.

Stinky and Fish squinted at him.

"It's almost ten," Stinky said. "I'm going to bed."

Fish nodded. "I've got two breakfast meetings tomorrow."

"Come on," Rip said, grinning desperately. "Let's go back to my place and jam."

Fish chuckled. "I don't think my fiancée would approve of that."

"You have a fiancée?"

"Her name is Lisa."

"How *is* Lisa?" Stinky asked. "Is everything...resolved?"

"The doctors say her thyroid is fine," Fish said. "But it was quite an ordeal they put her through. She had to have a biopsy."

"That's so traumatic," Stinky said. "Please tell her I'm thinking of her."

"Thank you," Fish said. "That'll mean a lot to her."

Rip cleared his throat.

"So...are you guys...like...not into jazz anymore?"

"I love jazz," Stinky said. "I gave to Lincoln Center this year."

"So did I," Fish said. "I'm in the Patron's Circle."

"I'm in the Angel's Circle," Stinky said. "You should do it. Once a year there's a luncheon with Wynton Marsalis."

"What's he like?"

"Lovely."

"What the fuck is going on?" Rip said. "Why are you guys talking like this? What the fuck is happening?"

"Whenever you're ready," said the rosy-cheeked waiter as he subtly slid the bill onto the table. Fish and Stinky flicked down a pair of MasterCards and glanced at Rip expectantly.

"I didn't eat anything," Rip said.

"I thought you had sashimi," Stanley said.

"I didn't!" Rip said. "I didn't have a single piece!"

His voice came out a lot louder than he'd meant it to. Fish and Stinky glanced at each other.

"Don't worry," Stanley said. "It's on us."

Rip followed his friends as they headed for the exit, buttoning their blazers as they walked.

"We should do this more often," Stinky said as he climbed into a cab. "It would be nice to make it a monthly thing."

"Or at least bimonthly," Fish said.

He shook Rip's hand and hailed a cab of his own.

"Bye, Fish," Rip said.

"It's Fred," Fish said.

It took Rip three hours to get back to his apartment. The G train had deteriorated since the early 2010s. It had always been slow, but now it was downright decrepit, like a sick old man lumbering around in the dark.

Rip trudged up the stairs to his apartment, pausing to catch his breath at every landing. Eventually, he made it up to the sixth floor. He stepped over his pile of bills, snorted his last two Adderalls, and flipped open his laptop. It was getting late and he had a lot of work to do on his jazz blog.

ELF ON THE SHELF

There aren't a lot of jobs out there for elves. You can work in the toy shop, a nonunion hellhole, and handcraft Hess trucks until you get arthritis. Or you can become an Elf on the Shelf. For me, growing up, the choice was easy. I know it will be challenging to monitor a child's behavior 24/7 and report every detail to Santa. But I want the opportunity to leave the North Pole. I want adventure and excitement. So the first chance I get, I hop in a box and let them ship me to a Walmart.

I wake up on a boy's shelf in Tampa. His face is smeared with Hot Pocket meat and his hair is cut into a rattail. As soon as I see him, I start to wonder if I've made the right decision.

"Look, Tanner!" says the boy's mom. "It's your new elf!"

And she starts to read him the book I came with, which explains my background. Before she can finish the intro, though, Tanner says, "Fuck you." Just curses his mother out, right to her face. So I watch the mom to see how she'll discipline her son. But she just smiles and says, "You better behave, or the elf will tell Santa!" And I realize, oh my God, there's no parental discipline in this house. And this woman has brought me here to try to instill some order, but it's obviously too little too late. And as I'm thinking this, Tanner picks up the book and throws it against the wall. And his mom, in a singsong voice, is, like, "Pick it up, or Santa will find out you're naughty." And Tanner says,

"Fuck Santa." And the mom goes off to make him more Hot Pockets. And that's when I know I'm in for a long December.

So this kid's only ten, but he's already masturbating. And when I say masturbating, I don't mean "exploring his body." I mean full-fledged, to-completion masturbation. His walls are plastered with *Playboy* centerfolds. He also has unrestricted Internet access and the sites he visits are truly twisted. Like, "time to destroy your hard drive" twisted. At one point, while masturbating, he looks right at me. I try my best to ignore him, but there's nothing I can do. I'm physically incapable of turning my head or closing my eyes. It's the most disturbing experience of my life.

That night, I fly to the North Pole to report Tanner's behavior to you-know-who. And I'm, like, "Listen, this kid is naughty. There's no need for further research."

And Santa's, like, "Just stay on his shelf through Christmas, maybe he'll turn a corner, ho ho ho." And I'm, like, "This kid is a psychopath." And Santa laughs and says, "Nice try, Buttercup. But you're not getting the holidays off." And then he leaves for his next meeting. And I'm, like, oh my God, I've gotta go back there.

The next day, Tanner's friends come over. And when they see me on the shelf, they start making fun of him and calling him a baby. So Tanner, to prove he's tough or whatever, decides that the thing to do is to shove my head up his ass. Literally, just pulls down his pants and sticks my head inside his ass. It happens so fast, it takes me a moment to realize what's going on. By the time he extracts me, his friends are all laughing hysterically, like it's the funniest thing they've ever seen. Then they all take out iPads and play single-shooter video games in silence.

After three hours of this madness, one of the kids says he's bored. So Tanner grabs me and I think, *Oh fuck, something really bad's about to happen.* Sure enough, the next thing I know I'm being tossed into the microwave. The stench of Hot Pockets is thick in the air. Tanner hits a button and I start to cook from the inside out. My face turns to goo. My feet catch on fire. It's the worst pain I've ever felt, but part of me feels relieved. My scars are no longer invisible; maybe now there will finally be some discipline, some modicum of justice? Wishful thinking. When Tanner's mom finds me, she just plops me right back on Tanner's shelf without comment. How's that for parenting?

That night, I go up Tanner's ass again, even though it's just the two of us. What started as a joke has become part of his masturbation ritual. I realize that this is how it's going to be from now on. Every time he masturbates, I'm going to be involved. And there are still twelve days until Christmas.

Up at the North Pole, I try to get another meeting with Santa. But his schedule is completely booked. As I'm flying back to Tanner's house, I pass Rudolph the Red-Nosed Reindeer. And he's, like, "I hear you're going through a hard time. Listen, we've all been there." And I'm, like, are you fucking kidding me? You're going to equate what I'm going through with being "excluded from games"? Fuck you. I'm inside an ass three times a day, and if it's washed, it's a Christmas miracle.

I get through December by mentally leaving my body. I just learn to disassociate. When Tanner is doing his thing, I'm not there. I'm in a different place. I'm at the beach.

Finally, on Christmas Eve, Santa calls in all the elves, from all the shelves, for the annual naughty-or-nice meeting. Some of my colleagues have mixed reports about their kids (they've witnessed bad manners and unmade beds), but everyone recommends that their boys and girls receive presents. Then it's my turn. I filibuster for over an hour. I describe every crime in disgusting, horrible detail. By the time I'm finished, half the elves are in tears. Sugarplum is in the bathroom puking. Santa's white as a sheet. He hasn't given a child coal in over a thousand years, but now he's got no choice.

"So," I say triumphantly, "how many lumps does Tanner get?"

Santa averts his eyes.

"The thing is," he says, "I kind of already got him a PlayStation 4."

And I'm, like, "What do you mean? It's not even Christmas yet."

And Santa explains that he delivers most presents in advance and hides them inside parents' closets to save himself travel time on the big day.

And I'm, like, "Are you telling me that the most hellish period of my life was completely in vain?"

But Santa's already off to his next meeting.

Since then, I've been going around to high schools like this one, sharing my story. I hope you learned something today about perseverance. At the very least, I hope I've dissuaded you from becoming an Elf on the Shelf, if that was a career path you were considering. Thank you to Mrs. Gonzales for organizing this assembly. You've all been wonderful. Merry Christmas.

UPPER EAST SIDE GHOSTS

Mr. and Mrs. Carr had been dead for several months, but like most ghosts, they thought they were still living. Their apartment hadn't been sold yet. And so they retained dominion over their darkened, dusty duplex on Seventy-Eighth and Park.

Their days were somewhat frustrating. The heat no longer worked. And Beto, their favorite doorman, had grown unaccountably rude, ignoring their *hola*s and refusing to open the door for them. In many ways, though, life continued as it had before their deaths. The *New York Times* still arrived, occasionally, due to a computer error. And while the Carrs were unable to flip through the pages, due to the incorporeity of their fingers, they could scan the headlines, which was all they'd really done while still alive.

The Carrs rarely left the Upper East Side, finding the rest of the city disorienting. But, luckily, their neighborhood was packed with ghosts like them. On Sundays, they liked to host the Benders, a witty couple they had known since law school. The Benders had died in a helicopter explosion but were otherwise in perfect health.

"I'm sorry it's so chilly," Mrs. Carr said as she air-kissed Mrs. Bender.

"It's the same at our place," she said between shivers. "It's Con Ed, they're the worst."

Mr. Bender gestured at his wife's trembling rump.

"Look!" he said. "She's twerking!"

All the ghosts laughed.

"You know, that's a *word* now," said Mrs. Bender. "In *The Oxford English Dictionary*. A verb—'to twerk'!"

"I read about that," said Mr. Carr. "In the *New York Times*."

Mr. Bender sardonically raised his eyebrows.

"Beethoven gave us 'Ode to Joy,' Wagner gave us *The Ring Cycle*, and now Miley Cyrus has given us... 'le twerk.'"

The ghosts all laughed some more.

"There probably won't even *be* music soon," said Mrs. Carr. "If it's not an 'app,' what's the point, right?"

"All this new technology drives me crazy," said Mrs. Bender. "Why can't a phone just be a phone? And these new walls they have now. How you can just walk right through them. I'm sorry, I'm showing my age here, but I liked it better when you couldn't walk through walls."

The other ghosts nodded. They'd noticed the strange new walls, too.

"These Millennials use so much technology that their brains are wired differently. They've done studies!"

"I read about that," said Mr. Carr. "In the *New York Times*."

"Our kids are prime examples," Mrs. Carr admitted. "They're *obsessed* with their phones. Last week, we visited Lily's new place. In, where else, *Brooklyn*."

The other ghosts chuckled with recognition.

"She was so busy texting, she didn't even say hello to us. It was like we weren't even there. I got so angry, I grabbed her phone and threw it across the room."

"What happened?"

"She started screaming and a lock of her hair turned white."

The Benders nodded. They'd had similar experiences while visiting their own children.

"Speaking of Millennials," Mrs. Bender said. "We have to tell you about this party we attended." She nudged her husband. "You tell it, honey. I'll never do it justice."

Mr. Bender licked his lips, relishing the anecdote.

"So we show up, and it's Alice, her fiancé, and a gypsy."

Mrs. Bender squealed. "Ted, you can't say 'gypsy'! It isn't politically correct!"

"So this *gypsy*..."

"Ted!"

"She's decked out in scarves, and rings, and holding a crystal ball."

"I assume this was in Brooklyn?" said Mrs. Carr.

"How did you know?" Mr. Bender asked sarcastically. "It was in a neighborhood called Ditmas Park."

"My God," Mrs. Carr said. "How did you even get there?"

Mr. Bender's smile faded. "You know, I don't remember." He turned to his wife with confusion. "Do you remember how we got there?"

"No," said Mrs. Bender after a lengthy pause. "It's almost like we just appeared in the space, as if out of a void."

"Anyway," Mr. Bender said. "This gypsy—"

"Ted!"

"She says, 'There is a spirit in our midst. Do you know anyone whose name begins with *T*?' And our daughter says, 'My father.' And I'm thinking, *What is this? What's going on?* So I try to talk to Alice, but she's giving us the silent treatment, as usual.

So I say to the gypsy, 'Will you please tell Alice to retake the GREs and I'll pay for it? Because that's been a source of contention between us for some time.' And the gypsy repeats what I've said, and Alice starts to cry. And she says, 'Dad, please, we might never get another chance to communicate. I want you to know that I love you.'" He shook his head in bafflement. "It's these new drugs kids are taking. They're much stronger than the ones we dabbled in. 'Molly.' That's one of them."

Mr. Carr nodded. "I read about that in the *New York Times*."

The door creaked open.

"Speak of the devil!" Mrs. Carr said as her two adult children, Lily and Brent, entered the apartment. She tried to hug them, but they slipped right through her arms.

"I'll do this closet," Lily told her brother. "You do that one."

Mrs. Carr watched in confusion as her children rifled through her old belongings.

"I'm sorry," she whispered to the Benders. "They're not usually this rude."

Mrs. Bender shrugged. "Our kids are the same way."

The ghosts tried to move their conversation forward to other interesting topics, like Obama and the new Woody Allen movie. But it was difficult to ignore the two rummaging Millennials.

"Remember this thing?" Lily asked, handing her brother a dusty Etch A Sketch.

"Sort of," he said. There were traces of an image on the screen: a few faint clouds and a wispy stick figure.

The ghosts were silent for a while.

"I love your new ceiling," Mrs. Bender said finally.

Mrs. Carr looked up and gasped. The crown molding was gone, replaced by a shapeless, throbbing whiteness. She couldn't remember when the men had come to install it.

"Should we go to it?" she asked softly.

"I think so," said Mr. Carr. They took each other's hands, and the Benders instinctively did the same. The four ghosts floated upward, past the wine racks and the bookshelves. Mrs. Carr glanced down at her son, Brent, and was surprised to see a bald spot in the middle of his scalp.

"I think we're ghosts," she said. And for the first time, they all understood the situation.

"Well," Mr. Bender said, raising an eyebrow. "I suppose this gives new meaning to the expression 'YOLO'!"

The ghosts smiled uneasily, confused by the reference.

"Or is it 'FOMO'?" Mr. Bender said. "Is it 'YOLO' or 'FOMO'?"

His wife kissed him gently on the cheek. "It doesn't matter, love."

The ghosts closed their eyes and melted pleasantly into a ball of crystal light.

"Did it get warm all of a sudden?" Lily asked.

"Yeah," her brother said. "I'm sweating."

Lily raised her eyebrows. "Climate change. They say this is the hottest January on record."

"I think I read about that," said Brent. "In the *New York Times*."

BIG BREAK

Tim was tuning his guitar backstage when he noticed something odd.

"Holy shit," he said. "Look."

Sanjay strolled over, drumsticks in hand.

"What's up?"

Tim pointed shakily through a gap in the curtains.

"Have you ever seen anything like that before?"

Sanjay's eyes widened.

"Not at one of *our* shows."

Tim could feel his heart speeding up and time slowing down. It was just like he'd always imagined it. An empty chair, in the center of the bar, with a paper sign taped to the seat.

RESERVED

"Who do you think it's for?" asked Pete, the keyboardist. "Fat Possum? Merge? Gigantic?"

"Indie labels don't reserve seats like that," Sanjay said. "It's probably someone from a major."

"It could be anyone," Tim said, trying his best to stay calm. "Anyone from anywhere."

The house music faded as the lights went down. Tim secured a daffodil to his lapel. He'd been employing this good-luck ritual since their very first show. Now, it seemed, it was finally paying dividends.

"This is it," he told his bandmates. "We've waited five years for this. Don't blow it."

As the curtain creaked open, Tim thought about how far the band had come. When they'd first started out, as seniors at Yale, they barely had enough songs for an EP. Now, the Fuzz had four self-released LPs under their belt. Their latest single — a reggae-inflected surf tune — had amassed more than twenty-five thousand plays on SoundCloud. And when they'd needed to raise five thousand dollars to record their latest album, they'd gotten it on Kickstarter in less than twenty days. No one had ever come to see them perform, though. At least, not anyone important.

Tim tried not to stare, but it was difficult. The talent scout was tall and frighteningly thin, in a form-fitting charcoal suit. Club Trash served only beer and wine, but somehow he'd gotten hold of a martini. He sipped from his glass and smirked at the stage, his lanky legs folded at the ankles.

"Hello, Williamsburg!" Tim howled into his microphone.

The crowd politely cheered. He could make out his mother's voice. She came to every show and her movements were as well rehearsed as the band's. She began each set with a loud "woot woot" and always shouted "yay!" at the completion of each song. At the end of every gig, when Tim announced their time was up, she booed sarcastically. Sometimes people laughed at her joke. Sometimes they didn't.

Tim launched into the band's newest song, an ambient tune

from their latest record. As he strummed his guitar, he spotted his stepfather, Henry, at the bar. His mother had clearly dragged him to the concert against his will. He was ordering a drink, his back to the stage. At Thanksgiving, after finishing his fourth glass of wine, Henry had suggested Tim apply for an internship at his consulting firm.

"I'm sure you'd be good at it," he'd said cheerfully. "And you'd still have music as a hobby."

The comment had so enraged Tim that he'd spent the next hour in his room. But now, looking back on it, he couldn't help but smile. What would Henry say if the Fuzz got signed to a major record label? He pictured the old man reacting to the news, staggering backward, spilling wine all over his cashmere sweater. It was such an absorbing fantasy that he almost missed his cue to start singing.

They'd played "Abel's Crossing" hundreds of times, but they still made occasional mistakes. Sanjay's drum part was complex — a jazzy 5/4 beat — and it often caused him to mistime his vocal harmonies. Tonight, though, the performance was flawless. Their voices braided together, in key and on rhythm. They sounded like professionals. Tim snuck a glance at the man in the charcoal suit. He was writing down notes in a small black book, his eyebrows scrunched with obvious interest.

"Let's play 'Love Monkey,' " Pete whispered.

Tim hesitated. "Love Monkey" was their most popular song to date. (It had been featured in a local car-wash commercial just two summers ago.) But it wasn't on the set list and Tim wasn't even sure he remembered all the words. Before Tim could make up his mind, Sanjay grabbed his microphone.

"This one's called 'Love Monkey'! One, two, three, four..."

There was nothing Tim could do but play. The song was supposed to be midtempo, but in his excitement, Sanjay wielded his sticks like a punk rocker. It was hard for Tim to keep up with him, but the chords weren't too hard and he managed to get used to the pace. Pete's girlfriend had brought her friends from med school, and when the final chorus started, they sang along with Tim.

Love monkey, I'm a love, love monkey!

When they finished the song, everybody went nuts, cheering and laughing and whistling. Even Henry put down his wineglass and clapped his hands with feeling. Tim eyed the man in the charcoal suit. He was typing out a message on his iPhone, his lips parted with concentration. Tim was trying to decipher his opinion of "Love Monkey" when the scout looked up from his phone and—shockingly—flashed him a thumbs-up. Tim turned to his bandmates. They were trying their best to stay cool, but he could tell by their grins that they'd both seen the gesture.

Tim checked his watch. The club had given them only twenty minutes (it was a Tuesday night and they were the first of three bands performing). That meant they had twelve minutes left—exactly enough time to play their magnum opus.

"Echoes Lowering" was the most ambitious piece of music that Tim had ever written. It was a meditation on music itself and the inherent difficulty of artistic expression. The song included a three-minute bridge during which the only instruments played were a toy piano, a triangle, and a purposefully untuned guitar.

It was during this bridge that Tim began to daydream about his future.

"Why the triangle?" Tim imagined a reporter asking him six months from now, in the penthouse of a European hotel.

"It is what it is," Tim would say through a translator.

"Do you enjoy touring? You seem frustrated by all the media and photographers."

"I just want to be back in the studio. Where things make sense."

Sanjay hit the crash, pulling Tim out of his revelry just in time to launch into the song's discordant outro. It was his favorite part of the album—an ironic series of power chords culminating in a blare of distortion.

Tim looked straight into the scout's eyes as he strummed the final bars. He played the last chord so aggressively that the daffodil nearly fell out of his lapel. When the song was over, he bolted from the stage without a word. What was the point of saying thanks or goodbye? The music had done the talking. Pete and Sanjay followed his lead, looks of intense stoicism on their faces.

The club owner was waiting for them in the greenroom.

"You only brought in five guests," he said. "So your take is ten dollars."

Tim chuckled. Normally, this kind of exchange would leave him shaken and humiliated. But now all he felt was pity.

"Was it difficult in the early days? I read in NME that you once played a set for ten dollars."

"That's a true story. But back then we didn't think about the money. We were just kids. Give us a stage and some amps, and we were happy..."

"Tim?" Pete said. "Do you have any cash on you?"

"Huh?"

"You each had two beers," explained the owner. "So that's six beers times four dollars is twenty-four dollars. Minus the ten, you still owe me fourteen. Plus tip."

Tim flushed.

"I thought the beers were free?"

The owner folded his arms across his chest.

"Beers are only free for headliners."

Tim rooted around in the pockets of his skinny jeans. His mom had given him sixty bucks a week ago, but he'd spent most of it on guitar strings. All he had left was a single crumpled twenty.

"Keep the change," he said, handing it over.

The owner grabbed the cash and walked away.

"Oh, one other thing," he said, spinning around suddenly. "There's some guy, he wants to talk to you. Says he's an agent. Asked me to tell you to meet him outside."

Sanjay swallowed.

"Are you sure he said us? And not one of the other bands?"

"Which band are you again?"

"We're the Fuzz," Tim said with annoyance.

"Yeah, it's you guys," said the owner. "He's right out front. In the limousine."

"Remember!" Tim said. "Don't sign anything, no matter what he says, until we speak to a lawyer!"

He was trying to act professional, but he couldn't suppress the childlike lilt in his voice. He realized he was happy, genuinely happy, for the first time in recent memory. He'd never admitted it to anyone, but lately he'd started having doubts about the band. When he first moved back home after school, he genuinely believed the situation would be temporary. He assumed he'd be on tour most of the summer and that, within a year at least, he'd be supporting himself with his music. It ended up taking him three years to organize a tour—a nine-day trek across the Midwest. And between the van and the gas, he'd ended up losing money.

"What's the absolute worst show you played?"

"Milwaukee. Hands down."

"Tough crowd?"

"Worse. Nobody came."

"What do you mean, 'nobody'?"

"Literally, nobody. The owner never promoted it and we didn't sell a single ticket."

"What did you do?"

"We played a few songs anyway, just for the waitstaff."

"Did they like it, at least?"

"They didn't even make eye contact with us. You could tell they were embarrassed that we were playing to an empty room."

"Did you ever think about giving up?"

"Never. When you believe in your music, nothing can stop you."

The limo was long, black, and gleaming. Tim was debating whether or not to knock when the door swung open automatically.

"Come in," said the man in the charcoal suit. Tim, Pete, and Sanjay climbed into the backseat. It was too dark to see. The only source of light was the man's cigar, a gleaming ring of fire casting shadows everywhere.

"I've been watching you for some time," the man said between puffs. "I think that's the best you've ever played."

Tim smirked at Pete. He'd always been the naysayer in the group, the one who threatened to pursue other projects. Now he was smiling like a five-year-old at Christmas.

"Do you know who I work for?" asked the man.

The bandmates looked at each other.

"Capitol?" Sanjay ventured.

"No."

"Atlantic?"

"No."

"Are you from an indie?" Tim asked, trying to mask his disappointment.

The thin man laughed.

"You kids are way off."

He picked up a crystal decanter and poured out a round of scotches.

"I'm sorry, I'm confused," Tim said. "Ralph said you were an agent."

"That guy is hard of hearing," he said, handing Tim a giant tumbler. "Hasn't got long to live, you know. Two years, five weeks, and a day."

The boys stared at the man in silence.

"I'm not an agent," he said. "I'm an *angel*. Can you guess which kind?"

He pointed a spindly finger at Tim's heart.

"Here's a hint."

Sanjay gasped as the daffodil in Tim's lapel began to wilt. The petals browned and crumpled into dust.

Tim glanced at Pete. He wasn't much of a drinker, but he'd already finished his scotch.

"Please," he whispered. "I don't want to die. Please, please . . ."

The angel held up a pale palm.

"Relax," he said. "I'm not here to kill you."

"Then why are you here?" Tim asked, a slight edge in his voice.

"To kill your dreams."

He topped off Pete's scotch.

"It's a new thing I'm doing," he explained. "Claiming lives is depressing. I mean, it can be fun, in a 'gotcha' sort of way. But it doesn't do the person any good. By the time I show up at a guy's doorstep, it's too late for him to change his ways. That's why I've decided, pro bono, to tell people when their dreams have definitively died. So they can move on with their lives."

"We're not quitting," Tim said through gritted teeth. "Music is our life."

Death smiled sympathetically.

"Did you know Sanjay's applying to law school?"

Tim glared at his drummer. "Is that true?"

"I was going to tell you," Sanjay said.

"And he's definitely getting in," the angel continued. "He spanked the LSATs Saturday."

"What did I get?" Sanjay asked.

"One seventy-six."

"Holy shit!" Sanjay shouted, bursting into laughter. "Holy crap!"

"You can still stay in the band," Tim pleaded. "You can go to Columbia and we'll work around your schedule."

"He's going to Yale," Death said.

Sanjay began to dance.

"You can't do this," Tim begged his drummer. "What about our fans?"

"You have no fans," Death informed him.

"Oh yeah?" Tim said. "Then how did we raise five thousand dollars on Kickstarter?"

"All the money came from Pete's mom's bridge club."

Tim winced. He'd always wondered why they had such a large Boca Raton fan base.

"Pete's going into finance," Death told Tim. "He's already been through four rounds of interviews."

"I was going to tell you," Pete said.

Tim's eyes filled with bitter tears.

"What am I going to do?" he asked, his voice as small as a child's.

"You'll work at an SAT-test-prep company," Death said. "The one Sanjay's sister runs."

"Oh my God!"

"It's not so bad," Death said. "It's where you'll meet Rachel."

"Who's Rachel?"

"Your wife."

Tim's sobbing slowed to a stop. He'd never had a serious girlfriend before. He'd always been too focused on his music.

"What's she like?" he asked.

"She's cool," Death said. "You'll like her."

"Will I still play music?"

"Not for a while," Death said. "You'll be so busy with work, you won't really have time for any hobbies. But in your forties, you'll form a cover band with your brother-in-law and do some free shows at local bars. Your daughter will be embarrassed by it, but then later, at her wedding, she'll ask you to play 'Forever Young.' Everyone will cry. It'll be a nice moment for you."

Tim nodded slowly. It did sound like a pretty nice moment.

"What's my cover band called?" he asked.

"The Fuzz!" Death said. "It's a great name. The name was never the problem."

Tim smiled with pride.

"Wish I could stay and chat," Death said. "But I'm running late. Gotta hit up some open-mic poetry shows in Tribeca."

The boys respectfully exited the limo.

"See you when I see you!" Death called out.

Tim sighed with relief as the black car sped away. He checked his watch. It was still early.

ACKNOWLEDGMENTS

I want to thank my incredibly patient agent, Daniel Greenberg, for reading all my work these past ten years. I don't know where I'd be without him.

I also want to thank Laura Tisdel and all the other wonderful editors who took the time to help me with these stories. They are: Susan Morrison, Lizzie Widdicombe, Emma Allen, Michael Agger, Rebecca Gray, Dan Abramson, Daniel Wenger, and Gail Winston (who doubles as both an editor and my mother).

I'm also extremely grateful to Reagan Arthur, Elizabeth Fisher, Tim Wojcik, Lee Eastman, Gregory McKnight, Ruth Petrie, Amanda Lang, Hannah Westland, Karen Landry, Jake Luce, Flora Willis, Anna-Marie Fitzgerald, and Brent Katz.

Most of all, I want to thank my brilliant, supportive, and supercool wife, Kathleen Hale. Meeting her remains by far the luckiest break of my life.

Reading Group Guide

SPOILED BRATS

Stories

BY SIMON RICH

An online version of this reading group guide is available at littlebrown.com.

Simon Rich on guilt, humor writing, and being the worst person ever

An interview by Jessica Gross

How old were you when you started actively, seriously writing?

Well, I always loved to write. As early as kindergarten, I plagiarized Roald Dahl stories that I would try to pass off as my own. But I think it sort of shifted around when I was seventeen. That's when I started writing every single day, whether or not I had an idea. Until then, I would sit down and write a story only if one occurred to me, and then I started to wake up every single day and write for a few hours whether or not I had anything worthwhile to say.

What was the impetus for doing that?

It was because I wanted to write a novel. I wrote a novel that I finished the summer after I graduated from high school—it was a terrible, terrible novel—but I knew I was going off to college and I assumed I would be too busy to write a whole book, so I decided I would finish it before I got to college. But a novel has a lot of pages, so I knew I would have to work every single day. When the summer was over, I had failed in writing a good novel, but I had succeeded in learning how to be a writer.

And you've just kept up that habit ever since?

Yeah, and gradually, over the course of years and years, the writing got a little bit better.

Do you ever have a day when you sit down to write and it's just not happening?

I always find something to write about. I mean, you always have some emotion inside of yourself. Sometimes the only emotion you feel is shame or disgust or embarrassment or whatever—it's not always the sexiest emotion—but as a living, breathing person, you always have something going on inside your brain and inside your heart. There's always something you can write about.

Your stories are so richly imaginative and kind of outlandish. Do you find that you're the kind of person who daydreams a lot? Do these scenarios occur to you in your nonwriting life, or is it a very disciplined thing where you're sitting down and thinking, "What's a scenario that would embody this emotion?"

I occasionally will suddenly have an idea out of nowhere—in the stereotypical Hollywood way, inspiration will strike—but that probably accounts for 5 or 10 percent of all my published work. The rest is the result of brute force.

So what does that mean, "brute force"? When you're sitting there, how do you actually go about brainstorming something that is so far out?

3

It's all about finding the right angle, right? Because none of the stories I tell are particularly original, and none of the themes I write about are new, and certainly, hopefully, none of the emotions I'm writing about are unique. So it's just about coming up with an original creative angle. So with "Sell Out," I don't think I'm the first person to wonder what it would be like to meet his ancestors. I mean, there's hundreds of works of art about it—everything from *Back to the Future* to *Time and Again* deals with those issues—so it was just about trial and error, systematically telling the story in every conceivable way until I found one that felt fresh and interesting and honest. Or the story "Unprotected" in my last book—I mean, how old a story can you tell? A teenage boy who wants to lose his virginity: it's the premise behind dozens of popular films. So it was just about, what's an original, creative, and visceral way to tell this old story of a teenage boy trying to get laid?

There are two Simon Rich characters in Spoiled Brats—*a kid in "Animals" and a late-twenties man in "Sell Out"—and they're both very unlikable. How great of a distortion is each?*

I would say that the book is embarrassingly autobiographical. I think those negative portrayals of Simon Rich are, I would say, shamefully accurate.

So the kid who appears in "Animals" is kind of a chubby monster—

Yeah, he's referred to as a monster by the hero of the story, the class hamster, and I think the hamster calls it like he sees it. I don't think any of his opinions of Simon Rich are off base.

4

Earlier stories in which you've had a Simon Rich character tend to be told in first person. Why have you moved into a third-person perspective for these?

It's become something of a postmodern trope to make yourself a character in your books. It's been done more and more with every passing decade, from Martin Amis to Jonathan Safran Foer. I always thought it would be more fun to make myself the villain than the hero. It just seemed like a more creatively interesting idea. And if you've made yourself the villain, it's more fun to write about yourself in the third person, because then you can really have at it.

How much of these harsh portrayals is an attempt to draw the reader in with an appealing level of self-deprecation, and how much comes from some real self-loathing or embarrassment or guilt?

This is definitely, by far, the most self-loathing book I've ever written. I mean, the book is called *Spoiled Brats*, and I'm the main villain. But I'm hopeful that some of the readers will relate to the characters in the stories and see something of themselves in them. I mean, the character of Simon Rich in the book is extremely narcissistic and self-absorbed and egomaniacal, and I think everybody has a little bit of that in them.

In "Animals," it's Simon Rich's turn to take care of the class hamster, and he blows it off. Did you have pets as a kid?

Yeah, I had classroom pets, hamsters, and I treated them terribly. It was my job to feed them occasionally, and I almost always forgot. My focus at the age of seven and eight was really just to watch television and sitcoms and then repeat the catchphrases as loudly as I possibly could. That was the fundamental goal of my existence for that period of my life.

In the story, Simon's choice phrase is "Whatchu talkin' 'bout, Willis?" Was that yours, too?

"Whatchu talkin' 'bout, Willis?" was up there, but I remember quoting *The Simpsons* ad nauseam, and everything from *Harry and the Hendersons* to *The Hogan Family*. I quoted everything that was in that box. The magical box.

The kids in Simon's class in the story seem to really take a shine to this habit—did you get that reaction?

You know, it's hard to know, because I had such little self-awareness at that age. I think at the time I probably thought that everything I was saying was hilarious.

At what age did you start to view that behavior as embarrassing?

I would say my late twenties.

Your writing has very surprising subversions that come fast and often, which lend a lot of comedy to it, but I feel like the humor is also often tied to linguistic details. So, for example, in that story, Simon is crying after the hero, the hamster, bites him. The whole setup is great, but the part that made me cackle was the hamster's line, in remembering his moment of glory: "I smile proudly, thinking of this scene." The formality of expression—

Yeah, it was very important to me to give the hamster high status, because he's so downtrodden and put-upon. It's just a basic comedy rule: if you're going to strip somebody of his dignity, you want him to start off as high status as possible. Not to get too technical about it—I mean, dissecting comedy is always the most boring thing in the world. There's no better way to ruin comedy than to talk about it. But yeah, if you're going to throw a pie in someone's face, you want it to be a man in a tuxedo, not a homeless person. So for that reason it was important, comedically, to make the hamster formal, articulate, eloquent, and high status, and so I gave him verbiage that I thought would bolster that.

I know it's a cliché that deconstructing a joke ruins it, but to me, the way comedy works is so mysterious, and I love having it explained. Are you saying that it ruins the joke for the person hearing it, or do you personally prefer not to be deconstructing comedy in this way?

I don't mind talking about it; I just feel bad for people who have to listen. But obviously, like all comedy nerds, I'm a student of comedy, I grew up obsessing over joke structure and trying to figure out why the things that made me laugh were making me laugh. In the writers' room at my show we spend hours and hours deconstructing jokes and gags and premises, trying to make them work more efficiently. So it's like anything else—it's like cooking or doing magic tricks or playing baseball: there's a lot of technical thought that goes into the construction, and it's very learnable. Anyone can learn these tricks, I'm convinced.

It's interesting that it comes down to such logical components, when the experience of hearing or reading comedy doesn't feel that way at all.

Yeah, there's a technical aspect to all creative pursuits. Even the most experimental abstract expressionists have to stretch a canvas, right? I mean, there's a lot of technical busywork that goes into the construction of any creative medium. But it's learnable. It's not that hard. I've got about five or ten rules of thumb that I keep in my brain as I'm writing. But then also you end up breaking these rules, and sometimes a joke will work *because* it's subverting another joke form. Like the piece in this book, "Guy Walks into a Bar," is basically just one big anti-joke that subverts one of the oldest joke structures in the world.

So what are the five to ten rules you keep in mind?

These are some real basic ones, but you always want to end a joke on the word that will elicit laughter. You want to make—and this is just for me, a lot of people will disagree—I always try to make things as economical as possible. I always try to make the turn sudden. I try not to shift a scene gradually; I try to shift a scene dramatically. Clarity is extremely important—just like with a magic trick, if a person watching has been lost during the setup, they're not going to understand the payoff and they're not going to marvel at it.

There's a lot of societal critique in some of these stories, like "Gifted," which uses a wealthy mom's relationship with her son—whom she treats as a uniquely gifted child, although he is an actual, literal monster—to skewer class privilege and modern parenting. How much of that is a by-product of the funny story you want to tell and how much is deliberate critique?

You know, when I'm writing comedy, I try not to come at it from a political place. I've found that whenever I try to get a point across through a work of fiction, the story ends up being didactic, stilted, and propagandistic. So when I write a story, the main thing I'm thinking about is, will it be emotionally visceral? Will it grab the reader? Will it make him interested in the characters and make him want to turn the page? That's the main thing I'm thinking about, more so, even, than whether or not it's going to be funny. So with "Gifted"—I mean, it's not a new premise, it's essentially *Rosemary's Baby*—I thought that the naïveté and ignorance of the speaker, the mother, would lend itself to some suspense and also some good gags.

I was noticing your language again in this story, particularly this passage, about her monster son, Ben: "Once, during a Spanish midterm, he escaped into the Hudson Valley woods and lived as a beast for several months." Again, the premise is really funny, but it's that phrase, "lived as a beast," that really got me.

Yeah, "beast" is a great word, right? Packs a lot of information into a single syllable. I really like the word "beast," and I use it a lot. Often, with a book, I have certain favorite words that I use over and over again because they always make me laugh, and then during the copyediting phase I always get a list from my editor of words that I've drastically overused, pleading with me to use synonyms. I do, up to a point, but you always find the word "beast" at least a dozen times in each book. You'll always find "nightmare" and "horrible" and "sigh."

Sigh?

People are perpetually sighing in all of my books, because they're constantly exasperated by these terrible situations that I've thrown at them.

Were you surprised by any of the words you were told you'd overused in this book?

"Williamsburg." I was surprised how many of those popped up.

So the centerpiece of this book is "Sell Out," which I originally read on The New Yorker's *website, in which a twenty-seven-year-old Brooklyn writer named Simon Rich meets his great-great-grandfather, an immigrant who fell into a pickle barrel a century ago and was preserved in brine at exactly Simon's age. What was the very first bit of this story that you got down on paper?*

At least since college, I've been thinking and writing about the kinds of conversations I might have with my ancestors if they saw how frivolous and privileged my life was. And the shame and guilt packed into those conversations always made me laugh. It took me a really long time to figure out how to construct a story that would allow for those interactions to occur, and I guess I was twenty-seven when I really started diving in and trying to write my ancestors' story in earnest for the first time. It took me five or six tries to find the right angle, because with all comedy writing—all writing, I assume—you're constantly making choices: First person, third person, second person? Who's talking, why are they talking, who are they talking to? You're constantly making all of these decisions and having to be self-aware about why you're making them.

There was a version of "Sell Out" told from my perspective. There were two versions that weren't about me specifically, just about generic hipsters being visited by their ancestors. And ultimately I had to step back and ask myself, "What is making you laugh about this? What is compelling you to write this, what emotion is driving this?" And it really was guilt and shame. And so I thought, if that's what this is really about, then I need to have that ancestor looking directly at me. I need to give him the power and give him the agency. So then I started writing scenes with him just watching me, describing me, and I got a lot of comedy out of that. But then the larger themes started popping into my brain—the immigrant experience and the Occupy movement and issues of class and privilege and the American dream and religion and humility versus pride—and the plot gradually presented itself. And then it went through a bunch of other drafts; the plot kept changing. There was a time when I was going to do it as a full novel, but then I decided that parts of it were too bloated and I didn't really want it to be that long, so I cut a bunch of it. It was a long-ish process. It's only about seventy-five pages, but it probably took me as long to write it as it normally takes me to write a full novel.

How many pages do you think you wrote that didn't end up in the final piece?

Oh, hundreds. But that's typical for me. I throw out most of what I write. But percentage-wise, what I kept for "Sell Out" was definitely the lowest.

How do you approach writing a collection? Do you start writing one-offs for The New Yorker *and then think about what kinds of pieces would fit around them to form a thematically driven collection? Or do you just decide to put the stories you've written into a collection afterward and see what theme emerges?*

I find it impossible to write about anything but what I'm interested in at the moment, and my interests and passions tend to shift from year to year, so that sort of naturally lends itself to collection writing. When I was twenty-five or twenty-six, the only thing on my brain was dating, and that's why I wrote all those love stories that became *The Last Girlfriend on Earth*. And then for a year or two I was obsessed with class and privilege and turning thirty, and *Spoiled Brats* is the result of that.

There's this Fresh Air *interview with Carrie Brownstein and Fred Armisen in which Brownstein says that she very much embodies the Portlanders they spoof in* Portlandia *and that she's not above their behavior or making fun of them. So what is your life like in Brooklyn—do you act like the hipsters you poke fun at in your writing? Do you go to the craft-beer bars, do you take joy in the lifestyle?*

Oh, yeah, completely. All of that stuff. I'm a complete, full bourgeois yuppie, unequivocally. If there is a hipster on earth, it's probably me. I'm certainly as revolting and privileged and narcissistic as any of the hipsters described in my book, if not more so. I mean, there's nobody worse than me.

I'm getting that sense. So, to go back in time a little bit: you grew up in New York City, in the East 50s; your parents were divorced and you and your older brother spent most of your time at your mother's. Can you describe what the dynamic was like in your house?

It was great. I had a great family, really supportive, wonderful parents and stepparents and wonderful older brother, great teachers, really lucky in every single possible respect.

That's . . . wonderful.

Yeah, I really hit the jackpot.

You read a lot of Roald Dahl as a kid. Who else?

Yeah, a ton of Roald Dahl. I was obsessed with *Mad Magazine*, I was obsessed with sitcoms—in particular *The Simpsons*, but also everything on Nick at Nite, from *I Love Lucy* to *The Dick Van Dyke Show* and *The Mary Tyler Moore Show*. I raided my older brother's bookshelf and, through his library, found writers like Philip Roth and T. C. Boyle and Kurt Vonnegut. By the time I got to high school, I was really obsessed with premise writers of all kinds, not just comedy writers like Douglas Adams and Joseph Heller but also people like Shirley Jackson and Stephen King.

We get a sense in "Animals" of what you were like as a kid, and in "Sell Out" of what you were like in your late twenties. What were you like in high school?

Super-pretentious, showing off a lot, kind of self-serious, insufferable. But fast, really fast. I ran the mile and I was really good at it. So I was at least quick on my feet. But in general a total nightmare.

How fast could you run a mile?

4:50.

Are you serious?

Yeah — which is, by the way, not great for most parts of the United States, but in my insulated private school community, I was fast. But we would race against large public schools and just get our asses kicked.

Do you still run?

Yeah, I run every day. Six miles.

After you graduated from college, you worked for Saturday Night Live *for four years. The schedule there is notoriously punishing. Was it difficult for you, or were you just so creatively stimulated and excited to be there that it didn't matter?*

I was just grateful to be there. Obviously, it's a lot of long hours — you have to stay up all night once or twice a week — but you do get the entire summer off, so it's not as grueling as it sounds. You're certainly very tired by the time the show starts on Saturday, but you can also spend July and August writing a novel in your bedroom, so there are definitely harder jobs. I think it would be a lot harder to be a staff writer on a sitcom and work forty-eight weeks a year, nine to five, in a room. I think that would be way more grueling, personally.

You're writing a film based on "Sell Out" with Seth Rogen and Evan Goldberg. How'd you decide to work with them?

I've been a fan of theirs for a really long time, and I've worked with them before. I actually wrote Seth Rogen's first monologue on *SNL*. I think they're really smart, and "Sell Out" is so tonally similar to a lot of the stuff they're doing these days, so it just seemed like a good fit. I just trust them.

What can you tell me about the ways in which the film will differ from the story?

That's always in flux—it shifts from draft to draft. But there's a lot of stuff that works best on the page and there's a lot of stuff that works best on the screen, and when you adapt from one medium to another you have to really use the medium and think about the medium before you think about the material. That's definitely one of the things I learned at Pixar. The most famous and beautiful scenes in Pixar history have no dialogue, and the reason is, they're an animation company. So they're using the medium effectively. Whereas if you were working on a radio show it'd be a different story. So you have to think medium first.

I imagine that was a learning experience on SNL, too, coming in as a writer and then having to translate from a script to a staged sketch.

The biggest learning curve for me was going from a magazine and book writer to being a sketch writer. That was the hardest thing, because writing for performers is so different from writing for the page.

You're working on a number of other film and television projects right now, too—there's a film based on your novel Elliot Allagash *and a TV series based on* The Last Girlfriend on Earth *called* Man Seeking Woman. *Am I missing anything?*

Yeah, but you don't want to be the guy who—

No, tell me!

No, no, as a screenwriter, you never want to be the guy who breaks news. It's just...it's unfair.

I thought you meant you didn't want to be the guy rattling off your list of projects.

Oh, no, are you crazy? I'd love to brag about every aspect of my life. This is what I live for. If it were up to me, I'd be reading you my shopping list.

This interview was originally published on *Longreads,* longreads.org, October 2014.

Questions and topics for discussion

1. How did your age influence your reading of these stories? Do you consider yourself part of the groups being satirized? If so, how did you cope with this? Drinking? Meditation? It was drinking, wasn't it?

2. "Simon Rich" appears a few times throughout the collection, often as the butt of the author's own jokes. Why do you think Simon Rich, the author, would choose to do that?

3. Do you recognize yourself in any of these characters? Which ones?

4. When you think about it, isn't the ability to sketch three-dimensional bone altars at any age an achievement?

5. If you met your great-great-grandfather after he'd been sealed in a pickle barrel for a hundred years, do you think he would think you were pretty cool, or just kind of so-so?

6. In "Guy Walks into a Bar," do you think the genie might actually have been hard of hearing and just trying to cover

for himself? Is a genie who grants the wrong wish better than no genie at all?

7. A question from Simon's editor, who is in no way associated with the literary establishment: isn't Gabe going to law school a more sensible choice?

8. Would you be happy if Death showed up at your band's gig? He does have a lot of connections.